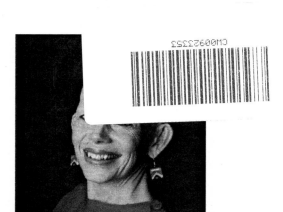

Sue Hampton is the author of more than twenty novels for children, teens and adults, writing across different genres. Michael Morpurgo has praised her work as "terrific" (Just For One Day) "enthralling" (Spirit and Fire) and "Beautifully written... insightful [and] poignant" regarding The Waterhouse Girl. Traces made the top three in The People's Book Prize 2012 and Frank won Bronze in The Wishing Shelf Awards 2013. Sue lost her hair in 1981 but it was creating Daisy Waterhouse that began to change the way she lived with Alopecia. Now, she's delighted to be an ambassador for Alopecia UK.

www.suehamptonauthor.co.uk

CRAZY DAISE

Also by Sue Hampton

Spirit and Fire
Shutdown
Voice of the Aspen
Just For One Day
The Lincoln Imp
The Waterhouse Girl
Twinside Out
Traces
The Snowgran / Ongalonging
The Judas Deer
Hue and Cry
Frank / Zoo and the Wannabe
Lap of the Gods
Start
Hail Neil / Headcases
Alas and Alack / The Troglin

Sue Hampton

CRAZY DAISE

Pegasus

PEGASUS PAPERBACK

© Copyright 2015
Sue Hampton

The right of Sue Hampton to be identified as author of
this work has been asserted by her in accordance with the
Copyright, Designs and Patents Act 1988.

All Rights Reserved
No reproduction, copy or transmission of this publication
may be made without written permission.
No paragraph of this publication may be reproduced,
copied or transmitted save with the written permission of the publisher,
or in accordance with the provisions
of the Copyright Act 1956 (as amended).

Any person who commits any unauthorised act in relation to
this publication may be liable to criminal
prosecution and civil claims for damages.

A CIP catalogue record for this title is
available from the British Library.

ISBN 978 1903490 90 7

All characters in this book are fictitious, and any resemblance to
actual persons living or dead is purely coincidental.

Pegasus *is an imprint of*
Pegasus Elliot Mackenzie Publishers Ltd.
www.pegasuspublishers.com

First Published in 2015

Pegasus
Sheraton House Castle Park
Cambridge England

Printed & Bound in Great Britain

This book is dedicated to Jen and Amy at Alopecia UK, along with young people like Chloe Jones, Charlotte Lenman, Molly Barker and Louise Hansford, who've inspired me with their courage, perspective and compassion.

I'd also like to dedicate *Crazy Daise* to the visionary and inspirational Polly Higgins. See www.eradicatingecocide.com

Cover design by Charlotte Lenman.

1

I'm Rowan so I'm named after a tree. Long before I met Daisy, I asked Mum why they didn't give me a pretty flower name like Heather or Rose. Mum said girls waste too much time and energy trying to be pretty when really they need to be tough. So she gave me a name that's strong. But eighteen months ago, she must have thought her plan had gone badly wrong. My branches were blowing around like ribbons and my roots weren't holding. I might as well have been Lala or Lace.

My mother, Julie May Figg, has no time for wimps. She's like an old Egyptian pyramid. She can't be shifted, and getting around her is hot and tiring. When I was little, if I argued about bedtime or homework, she'd say, "Jools rules!" with a forefinger aimed right at me. I wasn't fooled by the big grin. These were fights and she aimed to win. By eleven I called her seriously embarrassing. Other girls had mums who were soft and sympathetic but mine just made jokes and winked.

I'd seen photos of her wearing a dress, lipstick and heels, but after Dad left she said she just couldn't *be arsed with all that malarkey.* Even when she gigs her look is more Jo Brand than Beyoncé.

My mum has no problem with being a big woman. In fact she calls herself a Tardis, bigger on the inside. And that includes brains. Not that you need A Levels in Physics and Chemistry to work a fast food van.

"Is that like a mid-life crisis?" I asked her the first time I saw it. "On wheels?"

"Can't afford a Ferrari," she said, "or a toy boy!"

It was part of the switch from wife to single mum. As if all it took was a click – just highlight and delete. I thought that van was rusty old junk. It looked as if one kick would make it clatter into bits like Lego. But she transformed it, just like she transformed herself. *Reckless,* it says on the side, although I suggested *Death Sentence.*

"You're meant to know Physics!" I told her. "Doesn't *Jumbo Jools Saveloy* have the wrong kind of atoms? The kind that explode in your guts?"

"Only in Zac's," she said, and laughed.

Business has never exactly boomed but she's still there, near the recycling centre known as the dump, in her apron and cap. You can hear her even before you smell her because she plays Radio 2 above the hiss and sizzle, sings along and calls it rehearsing.

My brother Zac would live on chips if she'd let him. But he spends a lot of time chasing a football so he's not as fat as he deserves to be. Like Mum he's got a big voice and a laugh that makes you reach for the volume control. And for years he's been calling me Boat, sometimes with Rowan in front, as if it's still clever even though no one else thinks it's funny. Zac's never seemed bothered about having a now-and-then kind of dad who lives in another country, and the first time Mum told him about having to visit by Eurostar he just said, "Cool." I used to look at Zac as if he was one of those larvae you drag up in a net when you're pond dipping, another life-form. That's funny when you think what I became.

But even though it didn't look possible eighteen months ago I've done the same as Mum in a totally different way. I'm Rowan Figg remodelled. And I'm getting used to me.

When last year began, life meant school, shopping and coffee (shops) and *les vacances* in France with Dad and Mireille. I'd given up most of the after-school clubs I liked as a kid and dropped clarinet because Dee said it pulled my mouth out of shape. I'd fallen out of love with hockey because my lovely hair drooped in wind and rain and clung to my scalp like seaweed. That March my (well-acted) version for Mum was a sob story that I hadn't been picked for the team, when really I'd been dropped because I didn't turn up to practice. Luckily she didn't ask for an appointment with the PE department to demand justice. But I had a long lecture anyway, about *self-belief* and *commitment*.

"Rowan," she said, as my fingers tapped the keyboard, "you know how I feel about being phubbed."

"You should've got used to it by now," I said, eyes down.

She let that go because she thought I'd taken a knock but I was fine. I had friends like Dee and Yasmin. I wasn't short of boy attention and someone sent me a Valentine's card with a question mark. I hoped that was Aaron Detroit, because I sent one to him. I only dropped it in a post box after scanning the street like a cop on covert ops and then muttering, "OMG," to myself all the way home. Now that really is embarrassing. I think I only fell for his name and his hairstyle. According to Yasmin, he showed all the signs of fancying me, but he never said much more than, "All right?" when we found ourselves on the same stretch of corridor.

"Yeah," I'd say, as if I didn't care about him or anything.

I was just drifting. I'd never been the kind of student who sweats about assessments. I got by. Top set for Maths (thanks, Mum) and French (*merci Mireille)*. Second for English, though, so I could sit with Dee and keep our own sneaky sub-plot running with notes, looks, whispers and eyebrows. Teachers complained that I was 'under-achieving' and now it turns out they weren't wrong. But I was keeping my head down.

Until there was no way I could.

Sometimes I know things deep down but they're too scary to put into words, even in my own mind. I'd been noticing more hairs than usual caught in my brush and blocking the plughole in the shower. But I didn't say anything to anyone until term ended and I was meant to be packing for France. When I groaned about it – "I'll be bald by next week" – it was only like threatening to stay under the duvet because of a large red spot on the chin or a cold sore on my top lip. I was sounding off, not fortune-telling.

Mum took no notice. I always moaned and sulked about leaving my mates. In fact this time Dee and Yasmin were both away. And I'd just about stopped blaming everything on 'the *merveilleuse* Mireille' as Mum calls her. She's younger and thinner than Mum, runs her own *immobilier* business and goes to work in a suit that really is *chic*. That's how Dad met her, when she found him a property down south. It needed work but he's good at that, and now it's really lovely, like Mireille. So when she hugged me at the station I didn't freeze this time. I even returned her kisses – *deux*. She was wearing a long, loose dress and even though I noticed she was filling out a bit, she smelt good.

Dad strolled across the giant garden, Monsieur Take-It-Easy. Since he became a gardener (mainly for Brits with poolside holiday homes) he's had a permanent tan and hardly bothers to wear a shirt. I kept telling him that's gross unless you're half his age with a six-pack, but at least he has no belly overhang.

Zac always gets excited with a river just over the lane. Dad had already built him a raft, and fixed a rope to swing on so my mad brother could let go in the middle where the current is strongest. This time there was a canoe tied up and bobbing. Zac was in it before Dad started Step 2 of the instructor's health and safety tips. I took a photo of him waving a paddle like a weapon and grinning.

Mireille asked if I wanted to freshen up, possibly because my top was glued to my back. When I arrive each summer it always feels like fifty degrees in the shade. The shower is just one end of the bathroom, past the bidet, and when you've finished you mop the water across the tiles and down a kind of grating. Only I noticed the floor wasn't draining properly because the hole was blocked – with my hair. I had to turn off the shower and pick it all out, which felt gross. In the mirror when I faced it, I only looked horribly white and flat-headed.

I was blow-drying when Mireille floated in and offered me a French plait. "Your hair has grown so long," she said. Even when she makes a pointless comment like that, she still sounds classy.

The styling offer wasn't one I was likely to hear at home.

"*Merci beaucoup*," I said, and she started. A breeze stirred the long curtains at the French doors but I felt as if my whole body had soaked up the dry heat.

"I've been losing a lot of hair," I said, about the same moment she stopped brushing.

"Yes," she said. That was all. One word can tell you plenty. There was a kind of hush in it. "You haven't been pulling it, Rowan?"

"What? No!" I cried. "Show me? I want to see."

The lounge has a mirror, a big one I hated because it made me feel like I was on film all the time, but didn't know my lines. She jiggled a hand mirror until I saw what she'd found. Right in the centre there was a hairless patch of pink scalp, bigger than a biscuit. Mum could have fitted a burger on it.

Mireille said all the right things but I didn't hear them. I was staring at the back of my own head just like I'd look at a dead badger in the road.

"It'll grow back," I said, and my voice wobbled, "won't it?"

I was asking an estate agent! If I'd been talking to Mum I would have yelled something dramatic with *never* in it, and run to my room. I just wanted Mireille to tell me it would be OK so I could believe her because she's *merveilleuse*.

"You need to talk to your dad, Rowan," she told me. "Your mum too, for sure."

"I don't talk," I said, and gave her a tight smile. "*Je ne parle pas*." That meant full stop. Subject over. I reached for my brush and she let it go. "I'm tired," I said. "I'm going to lie down."

"I'll find out," said Mireille, "what it could be and what we can do."

"Don't do anything," I told her, with the voice of a toddler who's just landed face-first in the sandpit.

All I had to say up in my room was the obvious swear word but I beat that around like a squash player going for a world title. I felt angry now. As if it was someone's fault, totally out of order, and I wasn't going to take it lying down. Even though I did lie down, and pressed my face into the pillow again and again because my head couldn't find a place to rest in peace.

He didn't exactly jump into action but eventually Dad was knocking on the door, saying my name not much louder than a whisper. I faced the wall and decided not to answer however many times he said it. In the end I heard him open the door. I didn't turn round.

"No point in assuming the worst, love," he said. "Try not to worry. If you're strong... you know, mentally, emotionally... well, it'll help. Stressing always makes things harder."

"You'd know," I said, sarcastically. Butterflies are more stressed than my dad.

He asked me if there were problems at school, at home. I think I said, "Just the usual stuff."

Then he asked about boyfriends and I told him that was none of his business. I could tell he was running out of questions. Dad likes explanations, even with Nature: reasons for plant names and bee behaviour. When he doesn't speak I guess he's thinking hard.

I don't suppose I'd made eye contact yet. I was good at ducking that and I think it was his punishment. The room smelt of cut grass now he was in it. Very quietly, he asked me to sit up and look at him. I can take my time too, when I want to.

"It's a bald patch," he said. "My dad used to get them. No big deal." I opened my mouth to object to that, along the lines of that being easy for him to say. But he added, reaching for my hand, "It doesn't show at all. You get prettier and prettier, really."

Dad doesn't do compliments. And I liked to think I was good-looking in a standard sort of way, so I muttered, "Thanks," and pictured my Granny Sylvie with hair that was still thick the last time I saw her.

"Mireille isn't sure it's the best time to tell you but I said you'd want to know. I hope you'll think it's good news." He paused, not quite smiling. "You're going to have a baby brother or sister – maybe in time for Christmas."

He probably thought I'd take it badly but I was glad. I just told him I'd like a sister (to *adore* me *beaucoup* but I kept that bit to myself).

A couple of days later there was a hot wind.

"Rowan Boat!" yelled Zac. "You've got a bald bit!"

Luckily the river was noisier than usual and the nearest neighbours are kilometres away. I narrowed my eyes at him.

"Go drown in the river," I told him, and muttered, "Little rat."

I hadn't updated Mum. She was away herself, on the Norfolk Broads with our neighbour Val. When she rang that night she chuntered on about lock gates, bad drivers who shouldn't be allowed on the water and being nicknamed Admiral Jools. Then she waited a moment before asking, "That bald patch of yours isn't getting any bigger, is it?"

I was too busy feeling betrayed to answer at first. She said Dad had told her.

"I'm not looking," I lied. "Am I supposed to be measuring it twice a day?"

It seemed about the same to me: big enough. I was trying to go along with the idea that stressing would make things worse. So I told her I was chilling as much as anyone could in sixty degrees, and sun is good for Vitamin D. I hated the idea of them all discussing me.

Mum asked whether Dad and Mireille had looked *Alopecia* up on the Internet because there was some 'helpful stuff' online. The word was new to me and I didn't like the idea of having some kind of disease.

"You can ask them yourself," I said, and called Dad. I left the house phone facing upwards on the sofa, and could just hear Mum saying my name like a question, on a loop, louder each time.

I might have called Dee or Yasmin for some pointless gossip but at Dad's place you're more likely to get a rainbow than a signal on a mobile. I went to the bathroom and saw myself in the mirror, looking hostile, as if I was thinking: *What do you think you're staring at?* I took my fingers to my head and straight away the air was full of hairs, pale and drifting. Some were left behind, wrapping my fingers like Cat's Cradle.

I had to find out and it didn't take long. At the back of my head there was a second patch not far from the first. I let out a moan. My mouth hung, my shoulders shook and I looked anything but pretty. Back in my bedroom I lay face down on the bed.

In the end I played myself some music but it didn't wipe anything. My legs forgot I wasn't two and kicked the duvet. Then I felt the wetness on my face and the pillow. My tears were hot. They shocked me because I couldn't remember the last time I'd cried without a movie to make me.

"Baldy," I said, and stroked my soft, pretty hair.

2

Over to the diary – even though it makes me cringe a bit, and feel quite old. I found it in my case and it wasn't hard to work out who slipped it there or why. No dates, just blank pages and a thick Art Deco cover. No word DIARY either but someone – my guess was Val next-door – must have put the idea in Mum's head that what I needed was space to pour out feelings. I put it by my bed just in case. And a few days into the holiday I wrote in it.

August 3rd

The first thing I see when I wake is hairs. They curl and cross on the pillow. Seven today. I could choke on them. Then Dad would find me *froide et morte*.

Wish I could sleep in the day too. I sit on my own in some corner of the garden with my music and keep my eyes shut. Do bees have to pester the flowers 24/7?

Mireille keeps trying. She asks whether I want to help her with the shopping or supper. Whatever. Who cares?

Tried to swim in the pool today while Zac was up a tree but it was horrible. I kept leaving hair behind on the surface like an oil slick. Swear to God I nearly retched. I used the net to scoop up what I'd missed, with the leaves and dead wasps.

Last night Mireille put on a DVD where some lovesick Victorian girl keeps a guy's hair in a locket. Mine gets binned, and buried with garlic skin and orange peel. That's all my dead hair is good for – waste. Now I hate what's left, nearly as much as I love it.

Dad's smile fades whenever he finds me. Then there's a pause while he tries to think of something to say about some flower or bird. Well I don't know what to say to him either, except *I'm scared.*

I could only get the Internet for about ten minutes today but that was enough. Facebook's full of posts about how *bored* people are. *My heart bleeds*, I wrote. *You should try it here. There's no proper high street for about a million kilometres.* And if I see another moronic dumb-ass selfie with great hair I might be sick.

****
****

August 5th

Granny Sylvie *est ici* and she's taking me away to Paris! She's so cool, how could I *oublie*? She wears lipstick to match red wine and she says she used to be wild. Now she ties her long, woolly grey hair in a bun tighter than her jeans. She bends a bit in the middle like the old people on road signs but it doesn't slow her down. And she talks five times faster than Dad.

He's told me next to *rien* so I made him answer a few basic questions like why she left my English granddad. (Not because of the bald patches?) He just said she was a fish out of water in Maidenhead even before Amelie died. That's Dad's little sister who never got to be my aunt. She found out she had cancer while he was away at uni. OMG SO sad! She was sixteen. Granny Sylvie headed back to France after that and Grandpa died a year after the divorce. Mireille whispered, "She broke his heart," but how can she know? It's not her family and she probably wasn't even born. And what about Sylvie's heart, losing her daughter like that?

Mireille doesn't like Granny Sylvie because she doesn't keep in touch but that's only because she can't do technology. She's way more interesting than anyone I actually know.

As soon as she showed up she said we're going to get to know each other at last, girls together, and have an *aventure*. Dad's glad to hand me over – again. He's got no *idée* what to do with me. My gran's the opposite of Dad. She says she likes being Dickensian and Dad says that means OTT.

That's all right by *moi* cos I feel *extrême*. I'm packed and I can't wait.

****
****

August 6th

OMG I'm in Paris and it's SO cool. Not the hotel. That's like the set of a scary movie. I wouldn't get in the lift – it's got a grille, it creaks and you can see the cables. I took the stairs and found Granny Sylvie lying on one of the beds with ballet arms stretching out. The walls are dark red velvet with black swirls, very *Moulin Rouge*.

It's late now, she's in the shower and I'm watching English TV. Hope she doesn't snore or strip off in front of me.

I nearly prayed in the car. On the motorways she whipped round *les autres automobiles* like they were slalom sticks in the Winter Olympics. When she wasn't talking, she boo-booped along to jazz with no tune. Sounded way off-target to me – which made it funny, but her voice has a kind of crack right through so it's sad too. She might get heckled in some of the clubs Mum plays but OMG she'd *certainement* see off the drunks.

I don't always follow her stories. Being in a conversation with Granny Sylvie is a bit like finding yourself in a spidergram. She must know what's at the centre holding it together but when you're dangling on one end of a leg you have no *idée*. I think her life's a bit scrambled now. Just like mine!

I've been sending friends texts like: *You should meet my French gran – she's totally crazy!* Along with *Woop woop off to Paris.* Not a word about the scalp. But I'm checking each morning in case hairs have sprouted overnight like cress in an egg cup. So far, *seulement* in my dreams.

Granny Sylvie's got old lady hair. L'Oreal won't pay her millions to toss it about but I might swap if I could dye out the grey. Think I'll plait it for her tomorrow.

I know why she kidnapped me. It's a rescue and I need saving.

****
****

August 8th

Sylvie took me to a trichology clinic. Total waste of *temps*. Didn't like them anyway. Plus I hate being treated like a moron. The treatments hardly ever work and I don't want to be strung along for nothing. It's like parents fobbing kids off with 'maybe later' when they mean 'no'.

Pointless questions too. Am I stressed?!! Like it's my fault and I had it coming. They even did some test in case there are too many male hormones! *Merci beaucoup* and *charmant*. As if I'm butch like Sharon Field in Y10 – Dee calls her Bert. Sylvie says I'm as feminine as a *fleur*. She's so great. I know she paid a fortune but she just said, "Pouf!" which means I'm worth it. But a Clio new from the *automobile* showroom would be cheaper than one of those deluxe wigs.

She hasn't asked whether I want a wrinkly old ex of hers to get hold of the hair I have left. The names she keeps dropping (actresses and *chanteuses* who owed their style to him) mean *rien* to me. They might as well be dead, and it turns out some of them are. Sylvie reckons he wants to paint her but she's playing hard to get. Does she mean nude?!!!

I have to trust her but part of me thinks, OMD. That's Oh Mon Dieu. I'll find out tomorrow.

****

****

I remember so many details I didn't put in the diary. Granny Sylvie's French was so fast I wondered whether half the time she wanted to leave people behind. It was like that when we arrived at the clinic. She sounded like she was demanding service.

Everyone wore bright white bodycon overalls with navy blue trims. A woman with waves of slick chestnut hair arranged on her shoulders investigated my head with perfect fingers. Then she reported to Granny Sylvie in French as if I wasn't there.

I understood most of the questions even before I heard the word *problème*.

"I haven't got any," I said, interrupting the answer. "At least, not until now," I said, and added, "*maintenant*" in my best accent.

Suddenly Slick Chick faced me and spoke English that was much better than my French: "Cover creams and sprays give the hair a denser, thicker appearance. But not for you I think."

She looked back to my gran and the French poured out again as she pointed to my scalp, lifting the hair. Sylvie nodded and I got the idea. My *problème* was too advanced/serious/BIG for a cover-up job. So I needed something called *microscopie*.

Slick Chick needed a sample so she combed my hair and murmured, "Ah, oui," when some hairs gave up without a struggle. I glared at them on the comb as she inspected them. Traitors, I thought. Rats deserting a sinking ship.

Apparently the sample could provide information. Then she talked about examining the hair shaft. I imagined a single hair coming up out of darkness for air, like a miner. I'd been down an old coal mine on a school trip and it was so horribly awesome I still dream about it sometimes. Now I wanted some air myself.

The white room where we waited was full of giant lilies in cut-glass vases. Sylvie loved drinking in the scent but I couldn't breathe. And I wouldn't drink the strong French coffee. It seemed a long time and half of me hoped for a *petit miracle*. Sylvie kept up her scattergun chat while I flicked through fashion magazines, all full of women with fantastic hair. That seemed a bit like shoving chocolate cake in front of someone with a stapled stomach.

In the end the only thing the sample showed was that my iron was a bit low.

"Pouf!" said Sylvie and I thought she was going to ask for her money back. "She's a teenager! She menstruates!"

So then we were handed over to someone else, a man with scientist specs who took us through UVA light therapy and infra-red technology or *electrotherapie*. It all sounded scary to me.

"Will it work?" asked Sylvie.

There were lots of long words but I gathered what they meant and it wasn't yes.

"Great," I muttered. "Might as well shave my head now."

It was my granny who mentioned massage. "To expel toxins," she said, "and oxygenate. Wouldn't that encourage growth?"

He said, *"Possiblement,"* as if Sylvie was mad but massage sounded better to me than being zapped with lasers.

"I have good hands," said Sylvie, wiggling her fingers as if she was limbering them up for action. She wore more rings than Jacqueline Wilson so I thought if she started on my scalp they'd leave craters behind.

We left the clinic loaded with brochures glossier than Vogue – full of glamorous wigs, extensions and hairpieces. I knew Granny Sylvie had cash to splash but the Beckhams would blink at those numbers.

"I don't need a wig," I said.

"No," said my gran. "You have perfectly good hair and I know what to do with it. Or at least, I know someone who'll know. He spends most of his time with a paintbrush these days but he won't have lost his touch." She smiled her naughty smile. "I suspect he's still a little bit in love with me."

August 9th

Today was *fantastique*. When I sat down on the salon chair I felt like a little girl and now I look seventeen at least. I'm catwalk cool. Guillaume looks a bit plastic and he smells like honeysuckle but he's *mon héros*. While he snipped he was talking *tout le temps* and making Sylvie giggle over her champagne. And his old scented fingers shook a bit. But what he did was magic. Sylvie smiled at him as if he could paint her any time he liked. I almost cried with joy.

I'm so *très chic* it's not *vrai*. No scalp showing. Just a mussed, tapered shape. A style like that needs new clothes to match. So we went shopping. I'm beginning to love my gran *beaucoup*.

I sent Dee and Yasmin a photo. If they could see me strutting my *(nouveau)* stuff through Paris their *yeux* would be like tennis balls.

Wish Granny Sylvie hadn't made me get her into the hotel Wi-Fi though. She found out those UV rays can make you sick, turn your skin a funny colour and increase your risk of skin cancer. I could tell she was emotional. I wanted to ask which cancer took Amelie but I couldn't, so I just told her I'm the total opposite of stressed.

"You're *magnifique*," she said, and dug into her make-up bag for liquid black eyeliner.

I'm even more *magnifique* now. She says I look like Elizabeth Taylor as Cleopatra. Mum would lock me in my room. Dad would walk past me in the street.

Sylvie poured me some *vin rouge* with dinner and laughed when I said it was disgusting. Then she asked who the Prime Minister is because she keeps forgetting. I told her Mum says he's not worth remembering.

I've just sent *mes amies* a photo of me with a large glass in my hand.

****
****

August 12th

I've been too *fatiguée* to write. *Trop de* culture! Yesterday we went to a cool art gallery with the pipes on the outside and lots of awesome paintings and crazy sculptures. The way Sylvie talks you'd think she's mates with all the artists. But Kandinsky and Klee can't want to paint her, with or without clothes, because they're seriously dead.

Today it was a *bateau* on the river, no breeze to disturb my style. We went to the dermatologist but only for back-up. I might never need any gel on my scalp and right now it'd mess up my cool hair. I just can't help admiring myself in shop windows.

I told Sylvie I don't want to talk transplants (infection and bleeding) so she cancelled the appointment. But I'm letting her massage my neck. It brings out the cat in me.

****

****

August 16th

HA!
Ever felt *stupide?*

****

****

August 18th

Sylvie says it might help to write it down now I've stopped crying. Don't know how. There IS no help. I know that now.

So, I've been afraid of washing my new-look hair. But I was starting to smell like a farmyard. I couldn't put it off any longer. Swear to God I handled it like a baby chick new to the world.

I might as well have used the old rake at Dad's place. How to block the plug and wreck the hotel's plumbing in about four seconds!

I stood helpless and naked, just staring at the mess and moaning. I didn't even cover up when Sylvie came into the shower fully-clothed. She turned off the water and wrapped a towel around me. I couldn't speak.

Then she sat me on the bed and blow-dried the rest for me, singing her scat-type jazz under her breath. From the front I still looked cool but I wasn't fooled. Not anymore. She didn't show me the back and I knew why.

It's all been TOTALLY pointless. Like a stupid game, just pretending.

I could have done without my *nouveau* confidence. That hope was dumb, *fou*. I was better off being miserable at Dad and Mireille's.

I told Sylvie it's not her fault and I love her. I do. But no one can save me. I'll always hate Paris now.

****
****

3

I didn't write the diary for weeks. And when I did, well... it's like the News, with no space for anything good.

August 28th

I'm SO sick of everything – including climate change. It's everywhere. The politicians are too old to care. They don't know what it's like to be young like me and looking forward to life on a planet in chaos.

I've got my own chaos already thanks. Mum shuts down at any mention of Dad and Mireille's baby. She's so busy supporting Val next-door I hardly see her some evenings when she gets back from work. Val's husband cleared off a few months ago and Mum seems to hate him but she won't say what he's done. That's apart from packing his bag when Val told him to. Val's so up herself. Plus she looks like she's lost her comb and I hate that.

It's been raining for days but that's not the only reason I don't go out. I might see people. My big fat Brummie gran drops by to check on me. She's always puffed and sweaty so I don't go near enough for hugs any more. I hear her chatting away to Zac but she doesn't know what to say to me except offer me cups of tea and calories. Today it was a massive cheesecake. Swear to God she wouldn't take no for an answer. So I said it's bad enough having Alopecia without being *obese* too.

She said there was no need to be rude or ungrateful. I said I wasn't and mimicked her accent a bit. I can tell she hates me now but come on, it's like French – you pick it up. I miss Granny Sylvie.

Couldn't Mum take a few days off and MOTHER me? I feel like wrapping up the hairs I keep leaving behind in a package, and posting them to Mrs Jools Figg. With URGENT in red letters next to the stamp.

****
****

August 29th

Brummie Gran had to go to hospital today about her blood pressure so Zac spent a lot of time next-door with Dario the demon boy. Until he came home steaming, face red as ketchup. Mum says Dario's bound to be finding it hard to adjust to his parents' split. But divorce is so normal. Alopecia's not. I don't know a single person like me, not in my world.

"I'd rather be at SCHOOL!" Zac told Mum. "SHE doesn't have to go! It's not FAIR!" My brother did actually talk in capitals. It's SO tiring!

Dee and Yasmin are back from holidays now. They want me to meet them tomorrow. I'm scared but I'm going mad at home. I can wear the red leather hat Sylvie bought me in Paris. It keeps the hair at the back tucked in place. I hope.

****
****

August 30th

I didn't see it coming. Today the four of us were in a coffee shop when Dee reached for my French hat. Nightmare. I'm living it.

****
****

That's all I could write that night but I still remember the rest, all of it.

"Let's try it on, then!" Dee cried.

My arm shot out to stop her and I managed to grab it back. I lunged so fiercely I probably seemed a bit psychotic. I'm sure I must have flushed as I stuck it back on my head.

"Whoah!" cried Dee. "Like possessive or what!"

"She's been weird since France," said Yasmin, as if I wasn't there – or they wished I wasn't.

"I haven't!" I protested.

I looked down at my phone as a text arrived. Aaron Detroit. I tried not to react but I wanted to read it by myself. At the same time I couldn't wait.

He was asking if I wanted to go to the cinema later that afternoon. Something must have shown on my face because I heard, "What?" and "Who is it?"

OK, I answered him, and told them to mind their own business. But then I realised I couldn't go on a date with Aaron or anyone else – just as I felt my hat snatched right away. Out of reach this time, in Dee's hand. She passed it to Yasmin. I could play netball better than them so I could have won the game if I hadn't felt three foot tall.

But I couldn't just sit there with the back of my head visible to the world, and I didn't. Instead I flounced out of the coffee shop, showing my friends my bald patch. Showing everyone.

Around the corner, against the wall that led to the car park, I leaned, gasped and started to cry. I heard their voices so I knew they'd come out after me but I didn't want to know what they were saying and I didn't want to be found. I tucked myself away by the back of some bins and waited.

A couple of minutes later when they seemed to have walked off in the other direction, I looked back into the coffee shop, saw my hat on the table and picked it up without making eye contact with anyone. My own eyes were hot and wet. It's amazing what a scene you can make when you're frightened of being noticed.

Mum had just arrived home when I got back. I could smell the fat and onions.

"You need to tell them," she said about my friends.

I said it was a bit late for that.

"Tell them everything. Facts and feelings. Then they'll support you." She looked fierce. "They'd better!"

"They won't understand," I said. "I'm too embarrassing. Like that fat, cross-eyed girl in Y11 with a double chin and a moustache."

My mother stood then and drew a deep breath. "That girl deserves respect, Rowan. Same as you, me, all of us. I didn't bring you up to that! As if all that matters is looking like Kylie or Cheryl Cole!"

"Yeah, well," I muttered, "You *would* say that." Meaning Kylie and Chezza had no competition from her. Then I hoped she hadn't got it.

"What?" she challenged me. I felt like a heckler about to get more than he'd bargained for, but just what he deserved.

I looked at my phone. "Yeah, I know, all right."

"It's not all right. Not when you're dissing this fat girl – you listening, Rowan? – exactly the way you don't want to be dissed! What gives you the right? What gives anyone?"

Mum was shaking her head and letting out air like a burst tyre. Zac came in, pulled a face and went out again.

"OK!" I cried. "I'm upset, that's all!"

"This girl in Y11 didn't ask for a moustache any more than you asked for Alopecia!"

"I know, all right!"

I felt mean by this point because that girl, Maddie Templeton-Adams, was really nice to me once when I was trying to find something in the library. Now I'd started to fill up again and we hadn't even got as far as Aaron and the cinema. I couldn't trust myself to tell Mum that bit of the story so I found the text and passed her my phone.

"Do you like this boy?" she asked after a few moments of working it all out.

"She LOVES Aaron Detroit!" shouted my brother from the hallway. "Is supper ready yet?"

Mum shut the kitchen door and lowered her voice. "I don't see why you can't go to the cinema if you want to. I'll pick you up. I can drop him home too."

She did seem to be missing the point but I couldn't really say, *"But what if he touches my hair?"* in case she went ape at the idea of her little girl being touched anywhere.

"I suppose you want me to tell him all about my Alopecia and the chances of me being bald by Christmas? During the trailers? Or while we queue for popcorn?"

"That's your choice, Rowan. You have to stay in control."

"But I'm NOT!" I yelled. "It's all OUT OF CONTROL!"

I ran upstairs. Lying on the bed, I started to text Aaron, deleted, then tried again, and looked up to find Mum knocking. Not that she waited to be invited in.

She said it was her way to get on with things – as if I didn't know that. Then she told me she was going to take the next day off so we could talk properly, and go to the doctor.

"Doctors can't do anything," I said. "There's no cure."

Mum told me to let Dr Divani do her job. And maybe we could do something nice afterwards. But I jumped straight in: "I'd rather just chill here."

No comment. Mum was looking straight at me and it was off-putting. She came across and sat on the edge of my bed. "About this date with Aaron Cincinatti…"

"Detroit!" I groaned. I wasn't in the mood for Mum's little jokes.

"Do you want to go to the cinema with him?" She didn't wait for my answer. "Because if there's only one thing stopping you, don't let it. You should go."

She laid a hand on mine. It felt firm and warm as well as big and heavy. It made me feel like a little girl.

"I can't," I said, weakly.

"You can," she said. "And unless he's some little shit, you should. Otherwise the Alopecia scores and you're a goal down straight away. Forget the hair. Stay on top."

"Like my hair? Is that a joke?"

"I said forget the hair! It's only got follicles. You've got brains. And soul!"

"I'm not you." I remembered her in action at a show, hips on the move, so embarrassing. But I knew she was right and I wanted to thank her, smile and put on my Paris clothes. I just didn't think I could.

"You're tougher than you think." She stood up and promised to bring a cup of tea upstairs.

Reaching up from the back of my neck, I checked on the size of the problem, and the thin wispiness of the hair struggling to conceal it. I sent Aaron a text saying I was ill and added, *another time maybe.* Dead casual, dead cool. Then I cried as quietly as I could.

Alopecia 1 Rowan Figg 0. Not just a defeat but a walk-over.

I was probably the first girl to turn Aaron down and I don't think he appreciated it much. I waited. No reply.

That night I couldn't sleep. I wished Granny Sylvie would call and make me laugh. I pictured myself with Aaron in the cinema: me oozing careless confidence, him telling me how great I looked. But I could picture another scene that was much more believable: him running his hand through my hair as he kissed me, and crying, *"Yeurgh! What the…?"* I could see his fingers clogged with my hair. Poor Aaron was looking just as horrified as Macbeth when the blood won't wash off.

I checked my phone but the texts were just from my friends, apologising. Kind of. *Hope you're OK.*

I figured there was no answer to that.

August 31st

I can't take much more. Or LOSE much more.
I've had enough and I've lost enough.

****
****

It felt like the next big episode. I woke up that morning to a clump of hair lying loose beside me, as if the handful I imagined in Aaron's hand somehow ended up on my pillow. I rushed to the mirror and combed through, holding the hand mirror to show the back view. But the clump didn't come from there. My hairline at the centre above my forehead had receded, like cliffs worn away by sea. There was a little bay of skin, paler than my French-tanned face. And my hair was way too short to conceal it.

Mum heard me whimpering.

"Most people won't notice," she lied, "if you don't point it out." Then she suggested getting a *nice bandanna*. That's what you call a giveaway. I said I preferred my hat but she wasn't sure I could wear it indoors. I knew where she meant.

"I don't want to talk about school!" I yelled.

At the doctor's I wasn't sure I could face anyone else examining my scalp. Our GP is softly-spoken and graceful with what Mum calls old-fashioned manners. She asked me what percentage of my hair I'd lost.

"Thirty-seven percent," I said. It felt about right.

"Surely not, Rowan?" objected Mum. As if I underplayed anything.

"Sorry," I said. "Thirty-nine point four."

Dr Divani gave me a caring smile and searched my hair very gently, as if it might dissolve. Then she told me how important it is not to worry about it and I resisted saying, *"Ha!"*

"Four out of five people with Alopecia stop there," she said. "Just patches. And it often regrows at some point without any intervention."

"That's encouraging!" interjected Mum, looking at me as if she expected me to grin and dance on my chair.

When Dr Divani said immunotherapy works by causing an allergic reaction that can trigger hair growth – along with eczema and itchiness – Mum butted in.

"I don't like the sound of that."

"It's not really up to you, though, is it?" I asked. Not that I wanted a lumpy red rash on my head. "What about steroid injections?"

"Into the scalp?" cried Mum. "Isn't that agony?"

"Not for you," I muttered.

Dr Divani didn't deny the pain part and looked a bit grim, as if she was imagining a series of injections into her own scalp. She said she could refer me but she'd like me to think hard and be sure that was what I wanted. Adding that she had to say she didn't personally know of any permanent cases of regrowth at the end of it all.

I looked from Dr Divani's glossy black pony tail to Mum's scrubby crop of copper spikes. A million healthy follicles between them and I knew they'd gang up on me if I said yes. Which would have fired me up to resist the pressure but I'm useless with pain and hypodermics make me woozy.

"So two out of every ten people who start losing hair end up totally bald?" I asked. Dr Divani nodded. "And do they get it back – ever?"

"In most cases, not," said Dr Divani. "Again, if the hair does regrow it's often only temporary…"

"Before it all falls out again?" I thought she could have strung me some more hopeful line that would help me sleep better and cry less.

"A lot of people find their own ways of managing the condition, with or without wigs," she told me. "There's a support group not far away."

I didn't want to hang out with bald people even though I supposed it might make me feel better about not being (quite) like them. Mum thanked the doctor and I managed a mumble.

"It's tough, Rowan," Dr Divani said, "especially at an age when it's normal to be self-conscious about appearance, but the best thing you can do is try to get on with your life."

That was definitely a cue for a *"Ha!"* especially when Mum said, "That's just what I tell her."

It doesn't matter how many people tell me, I thought, *I'd like to see anyone try.*

But that came later.

I know Mum wanted to help and I know that final day of the holidays was meant to be for bonding. Living with someone so solid can make you feel like sand and I quite fancied being washed away. I didn't want to talk about it and she couldn't tempt me out – even for shopping or food. There were people everywhere, people with hair.

So I claimed to feel sick. And Mum spent the rest of her day off checking up on me every half hour, only to be told I didn't want anything but tea. Except when I pretended to be asleep.

Later I heard Zac talking on the landing. "I could cheer her up," he said.

Mum said it was best to let me rest. The next thing I overheard, just when I was thinking he could be quite cute at times, made me sit up in bed.

"I told next-door about her hallo pea shirt thing and Val said it's just hair. She's not going to die."

My shoulders shook and I hardly had the breath to yell but I did my best. "You have no right to tell anyone!" I shouted from my bed. "You keep you stupid little mouth shut!"

Even though I nearly cried out that I wished I *was* going to die, I knew that would be pretty sick. Someone in the year below gave up school with leukaemia and no one expected her back. But that's reasoning, the kind they don't test at school. Feelings are different and sometimes they're cut off from the part of the brain that does sense. That's how mine felt, stranded.

Mum came in and tried to calm me down but I just turned away. The firmer she was about people meaning well and things being all right, the more I blocked her out.

I'd decided. I couldn't go to school.

4

Sept 3rd

It's not a lie. I'm ill. It's what happens if you don't eat or sleep. But I rounded up the temperature. And I stuck my finger down my throat for a good loud retch. She may not even suspect because she's not the sneaky kind. Zac does, I can tell. He doesn't call me Boat now because he doesn't like me.

How boring can a day be?

I pretended to be asleep when Gran checked on me.

Alopecia 2 Rowan 0.

****
****

Sept 5th

Change of direction. Aaron sent a text: *Get well soon.*

Those three words tell me a lot. Aaron's missed me. So he's a nice boy and he really likes me.

Thanx. Might be back 2moro.

No kiss. Then I thought: suppose it's got round what Dee and Yasmin saw when I stormed out of the coffee shop. Maybe he meant he hoped I'd get over the Alopecia soon. Which would be kind but horrible too.

Cool, he said. That's such a reflex it has zero meaning, even with the smiley.

Now I'm telling myself the same word. Not OMG, just cool. Wait and see.

****
****

Sept 6th

So I went back to school today and I hope Mum's happy now because I'm NOT.

****
****

That day started OK.

"You all right?" asked Dee.

"Yeah," I said. "Did I miss much?"

They filled me in on what they called the gossip and then got round to the work I might have to catch up on. Yasmin said she'd scan and email me her notes.

They knew *I* knew what they didn't mention but I acted as if nothing had happened. I didn't see Aaron anywhere anytime. I began to think Mum was right about overreacting. At lunchtime I went to the library to catch up a bit, just to avoid the wind outside. I wasn't prepared for Mrs Farrow, the head of year, to pounce on me in the corridor and ask if she could have a word.

I broke out of the teenage traffic to follow. She walked on, a few bodies ahead of me in her little heels and business exec suit. A few paces later she was heading out of the double doors into what's called the courtyard. It's really just the space where they didn't bother to join up the new building to the rest. On wet days girls run across it with bags over their heads, wishing they hadn't worn pumps.

As I tried to catch Mrs Farrow up I felt a gust tug my hair from behind. The coolness of my bare scalp told me it was on show. Slapping on both hands to press my hair back over it, I hurried back indoors. Then I hid in the loos. I don't know how long it took Mrs F to realise I wasn't behind her. I needed time on my own. I had to reassemble. Literally, on my head, and inside it.

I dug the least embarrassing bandanna out of my bag and tried not to cry when I passed a window and saw myself in it. I had to keep my eyes ahead when I walked into the lesson late. Top set Maths but I couldn't do any. I think the silence was worse than jeers.

Of course Mrs Farrow had no choice but to hunt me down. At the end of the day she was there at the classroom door and this time she whisked me along the corridor to her cupboard-sized office. It wasn't what you'd call paper-free.

When she told me to sit down, the files on her desk came up to my chin. Stuck on the wall I saw a photo of a girl about my age with great hair, smiling in a bridesmaid's dress. I couldn't imagine having a mum like Mrs Farrow.

"Rowan," she said, "your mother called."

"Oh God," I muttered.

"She thought we should know you've been upset."

"I don't really want to talk about it," I said weakly.

"She wonders whether it might be easier for you to tell your peers you have Alopecia, so it's out there and not a secret."

"That wouldn't be easy," I said.

"It's something to think about, if things... well, progress."

"OK," I said. "Can I go home?"

"Of course you can wear a scarf if you choose."

I didn't say anything to that. I just played with my fingers, wishing I could phub her. Then she offered counselling anytime I felt I needed it.

"Thanks," I said. "I don't."

I hurried out of her office feeling angry with Mum and Miss Farrow and the French trichologist too. No one seemed to understand that I just wanted to be left alone.

I wished I'd stayed in bed.

Waiting at the school gates with a friend who sloped off at the sight of me was Aaron Detroit, chewing gum. He didn't smile or wave, just looked, and the sun caught the gleam in his gelled hair.

"Hey," he said. "You all right now?"

There was an honest answer to that and my face probably showed it but I said I was fine.

"I thought you were knocking me back about the film," he said.

"No," I said airily. "I said another time maybe."

"OK," he said. He was looking at me like a detective with a suspect. "Someone just said you've got a disease that makes your hair fall out."

I swore but it came out wobbly and he said, "Don't get upset." Then he touched his own hair (carefully, as if he didn't want to wake it) and grinned. "It's not catching, is it?"

"Funny!" I said.

"I'm skint at the moment. Can't afford the cinema."

"Whatever," I said.

"See ya then."

But there were things I didn't want him to see. I wasn't going to walk ahead so I got out my phone, kept my eyes on it and pretended to be knee-deep in tweets until I felt sure he'd gone. Then I walked home, eyes ahead, listening to music.

When Mum came home I wouldn't speak to her for a while but she needled me into shouting at her, which turned into crying. In the end I let her hug me. She offered to massage my patches but I did that myself, as calmly as possible, applying the lotion from Paris first even though it did burn.

Then she said I could try meditating. I looked at her as if she'd lost her own plot and stolen someone else's. Val's.

"Great plan!" I cried. "A whole weekend to get Buddha on my side."

I plonked myself down on the floor, crossed my legs and hummed. When I opened my eyes Mum was waiting.

"Do you have to be so hard to help?"

I said sorry like a swear word and the knock on the door meant Val so I never answered the question. I knew I was zero fun. My moods were like those sound waves on the car radio, zigzagging all over the place. And I liked my own chart music as loud as possible, through the ears into my head and filling my whole body like an electric charge.

Just so I could feel something else.

Sept 17th

None of it works. Nothing can stop it. I don't brush these days but the hair on my comb is some kind of world record. I'm picking hairs off the sofa, the carpet, the washbasin and the worktops. I tell myself not to look but then I disobey my own orders.

I've started wearing my French hat to school but it just feels stupid, not chic. Today I tried eye liner like Granny Sylvie's and it makes me look like I don't care. Cue quiet word from Farrow. She understands *but rules are for everyone.* Hello? I'm not LIKE everyone. Isn't that LIKE the whole point?

At lunchtime a couple of runty Y7 boys on the corridors asked if I had cancer.

"NO!" I said. "All right?"

My face was twisted, eyes on glare. I don't need eyeliner to do Wicked Witch. They ran off as if I might cast a spell on them. But how does that work when they're like toads already?

Most of the time I duck it, even with my friends. Nothing's normal underneath. Blanking Aaron Detroit just got easier though. I saw him smoking and I hate the smell in people's hair.

Mum's been banging on all evening about some support group for Alopecia UK. They're meeting at the weekend and Mum's like a vulture with a carcass. She's not letting go. She says it makes sense to meet other people going through the same kind of experience. But out in the world, I like to pretend I'm not experiencing anything at all. Mum called the number and came back pleased because there's one teenager called Daisy who's a regular.

Yeah, but without hair she can't exactly be a regular teenager, can she? That's a totally different thing. That's all I want to be, the same as everyone else. It's like a human right.

****
****

Sept 22nd

I don't want help with false eyelashes. I just want to keep my own. I don't want to make a joke or an artwork out of my scalp, thanks. I just want hair, and plenty of it. Mine.

There's this girl Daisy who's sixteen. She's had no hair for most of FIVE YEARS. I've always thought that by the time I'm sixteen I'll have a perfect figure, great shoes and a gorgeous boyfriend. That's on top of hair that looks stunning whatever I do to it. And people will be well impressed, maybe even jealous.

HA!

I should feel less alone tonight because there's someone out there who understands and everybody seems to think she's some kind of saint. Mum's acting as if meeting Daisy's going to make all the difference. But the point is we ARE different. TOTALLY.

I couldn't be like her even if I wanted to be, and I don't.

****
****

Rereading that entry I can feel a resentment Daisy would have understood. The diary's full of big days that don't let you forget them but looking back this one was XL.

Mum drove to a town I'd never been to before, which claims (on the sign that greets you when you arrive) to be *historic*, but when we passed the castle all I saw was a ruin with no tea shop. As we edged along the high street I could tell it was upmarket: mostly boutiques, beauty salons and hairdressers, stalls selling artisan breads and olives, and not much smoking in the street.

Mum gave me a look when I said it was a Val sort of place. But the café is at the cheaper end. Looking at the shop front with its handwritten menu board and things dangling, I called it weird.

"It looks like a jumble sale in Abu Dhabi," I said. I had no clue where that was but I just liked saying the words.

Mum eventually managed to park on a hill between two massive vehicles, but only after scrabbling like a hamster on the wheel. "I'm in a muck sweat now," she complained.

The café door pinged as she pushed it open and let some incense out. No bald heads and no wigs in sight. Just a neat-looking family at one table and a couple of stylish women at another, one black and one Asian but definitely not losing any hair. Everyone said hello or smiled, and another woman who seemed to be the owner came to greet us with menus. Her head was wrapped in some kind of headdress but I guessed that was religion, not hair loss. She might have come from Abu Dhabi for all I knew and she was wearing a kind of long, colourful tunic over loose, wide trousers, but she sounded very English and full of enthusiasm. Anyone would have thought we were old friends reunited.

Mum told her why we were there, not at nightclub volume but still out loud. I knew I shouldn't have come.

"Oh, they're upstairs," she said. "Do go on up and I'll be with you in a minute." She gave me a bright smile. "Daisy's here."

Mum looked at me as if that was meant to be good news. I kept my eyes on my phone, which meant I stumbled on the stairs. It made me cross to think Daisy and co must have heard me – along with Mum laughing and joking: "Good trip?!"

Mum has trouble with low-profile. "Wow, Aladdin's Cave!" she announced as we looked through the door into the big upstairs space.

I didn't care about the décor, or where all the mirrors, vases, tablecloths and hangings came from. But I could see someone who looked right at home. In fact, she was almost camouflaged. The girl sat at the window seat, wearing a loose patchwork-patterned shirt over purple jeans. Her feathery hoop earrings were almost as big as her head. And that was outlined against the glass, completely bald. When she waved I saw her wrist was stacked with about twelve thin embroidered or beaded bracelets in different colours.

She didn't look sorry for herself. I guessed the woman next to her was her mum because she had the same smile, but she wore a little velvet cap and the hair that hung down underneath it looked a bit straggly.

The other woman, who was older and overweight, had a solid sort of wig with the wrong kind of glisten in the sunlight. I thought her eyebrows might have been felt-tipped on. Daisy said she was Frances.

She also introduced her mum, Molly. Mine told me to turn off my phone but I took no notice. Molly explained that Maureen must have been held up.

"Not at gunpoint, I hope!" said Mum.

"Coming!" called a voice up the stairs. "Not kidnapped by aliens after all!"

Then Maureen bundled in, pulling off her sunglasses and looking puffed. She seemed to be weighed down with a laptop bag over her skinny shoulders. She was bareheaded too, but heavily made-up and dressed up in a short skirt and heels. Her apologies were breathy. As she sat down I noticed the raised veins in her bare scalp. I thought the aliens might think she was one of them.

"I'm Maureen," she said, holding out a hand for Mum to shake. "You must be Jools and Rowan. Lovely to meet you."

It was warm with the sun shining in. I took off my hat. I suppose it was easier than usual because Mum and I had more hair between us than the rest put together. I felt young and almost normal.

There were about fifty weird teas with fancy names and although Mum usually says builder's is best, she went for orange hibiscus. I asked for basic regular and proper milk. That was the first time I ever heard of beetroot in cake but I wasn't in the mood to try it even though Daisy said, "It's gorgeous!"

All this took a while but eventually Jana read through the list and disappeared, leaving Maureen to look at her watch and say we might as well get started as she thought a couple of the others were still on holiday.

"Did you two fly off anywhere nice?" she asked Molly and Daisy.

Back then I had no idea caring about your carbon footprint could stop anyone flying like it stopped Daisy. She said they'd been to Bruges on Eurostar and it was amazing. Then she asked, "What about you, Rowan?"

I could have told her about Paris and my mad granny but it had all been for nothing. The mission had failed. As I didn't answer, Mum filled in with more information than anyone would need about Dad, Mireille and the baby, and the burger business too.

"I've got a baby godchild," Daisy told me. "Blonde like you."

"Probably born with more hair," I blurted.

That's the Daisy Effect. She brings out the things you usually hide. I was feeling the patches that were close to joining up at the back.

"You might hold on to the rest," said Daisy. "Some people do."

I asked her whether hers started with patches and she gave me the short version of the story. It began the same as mine but the next part scared me. Areata to Universalis (that means the lot, no body hair AT ALL), then regrowth. But not for long.

"I'm not sure mine's going to make another comeback." She looked at her mum, who was chatting with mine about food. "I don't think we're typical, Mum and me. So don't panic about your family going the same way."

"I'm not," I said, because it had never crossed my mind. I'd been focused on me. "I'm just scared."

She knew what I meant: of ending up like her.

"I was. Just don't bottle everything up." She mimed some kind of overspill. "It gets explosive. I was tougher second time round. I knew the worst had been and gone."

I wanted to know what the worst was. But then again, I didn't, no way. I looked on screen at stupid selfies. She didn't seem offended but Mum kicked me.

"I've decided it's not so bad being me," Daisy said. "And I'm me with hair and without."

She really meant it. The others stopped talking just at that moment and Maureen clapped. Molly put an arm round her. I noticed Frances look into her lap at her rather thick, old hands and I thought she might be close to tears.

"Daisy for Prime Minister is what I say," she said as she looked up again.

Daisy pulled a face. "I'd never sleep," she said. "So much needs changing."

She flushed and there was the kind of silence no one knows how to break.

"Well," said Maureen, "let's get the business side over with, shall we?" She looked at me. "I've got a few bits and pieces to scatter about in case they're helpful to anyone."

I didn't pay much attention to a fundraising event in Birmingham involving mad hair. Clowning around in a green wig is never going to be my thing. I kept scrolling through Facebook while Maureen mentioned someone being sponsored on a sky dive, even though Daisy said she knew the girl who was jumping and she was amazing.

And I couldn't see why anyone would want to look at photographs of bald women in an exhibition in London, or why bald women would want them to. But Daisy said she planned to catch the exhibition one weekend when she was visiting her dad.

"No one would pay an entrance fee to see me without this!" said Frances. Or with it, I thought, because she wasn't exactly a looker and the wig might as well have been plastic.

Then Maureen gave out little cards, explaining, "There's a beauty therapist just down the high street offering eyelashes and eyebrows half-price for Alopecia sufferers."

I realised I should be counting my lashes when I applied mascara in the mornings. I looked at Daisy because she had none that I could see. It made her face look really open. She leaned towards me and muttered, "I hate that word."

I looked blankly back.

"Sufferers," she said, "as if it's a chronic or life-threatening illness." Maureen glanced at her because the others had stopped talking about the offer. "But I can't think of a better one so I'll shut up," she said, in a more public voice. "Sorry, Maureen."

I nearly told her I *was* suffering. Mum was probably thinking about mothers of sufferers suffering too.

"I've tried to draw eyebrows on with kohl," said Frances. "I looked surprised, you know, like in a cartoon."

Molly said she'd teach her. They talked tattoos.

"I fancy a head covered in butterflies," said Daisy. "Henna, not needles."

"You look like a butterfly already!" joked Maureen.

More of a dolphin, I thought. Not just because of her bare head, but her build too. I remember thinking the butterfly should be me. I was lighter and prettier.

The rest of them were swapping stories and being kind to each other while Mum listened and made notes. Then Maureen started talking about an American who was collecting Alopecia stories. Frances said she could have hers, but it wasn't much of a page-turner. She seemed to think this woman in the States would like to include Daisy's but Daisy did a shy, coy, *oh no* thing.

Jana appeared offering free top-ups and Mum said, "I'll have a cardamom coffee, whatever that is – just for the hell of it!"

I realised that being the only one in the group with fully-functional follicles had kept her quiet. I thought she should feel guilty now for not taking better care of her dry, home-dyed hair.

"It was brave of you to come," murmured Daisy.

In fact I was afraid of doing what the others did, and using the *I* word.

"Maybe it helps knowing other people have felt the same?" she continued. "But not exactly." She looked around. "We've all found different ways of getting through."

"I just want to find a way *back*," I said. "Don't you?"

"I used to," she said, running a hand over her scalp, "but you can't reverse. That's like trying to un-live your life. Everything you experience can make you bigger."

I felt pea-sized.

She grinned and nodded. "You don't believe me now but it will."

She was all bright-faced with hope for me, as if she thought I had some kind of power over who I could be and the life I was caught up in. I decided she was from some other planet and you can't be jealous of an alien.

Soon the meeting was breaking up and before I could run for the car she hugged me. Or tried. I think I froze or shrank. She felt warm and one feather from her earrings tickled my neck.

"We've swapped emails," said Mum.

"And mobile numbers," added Molly.

"In case you two want to keep in touch," added Mum.

Cringe, I thought. I glared at Mum because I hoped she hadn't given away anything of mine. She did enough waving and calling goodbye for the two of us.

"It's not an arranged marriage," I said as we walked to the car.

"I thought she was inspiring," said Mum, braced-up against me.

"Be inspired if you want," I said. "I'd rather be Lady Gaga."

5

It's obvious now. What I couldn't handle about Daisy was my fear: that I'd soon be bald too, but with no idea how to live with it like she did. I accepted her as a Facebook friend but all her posts were about climate change, poverty and endangered animals, mostly with petitions thrown in. I decided not to follow her on Twitter. If I wanted all those depressing updates I could watch the News. She emailed just to let me know she hoped I'd keep in touch but I didn't reply for a couple of days, and when I did I just said *Thanx*.

She emailed back that she didn't want to be a pest but if I did want to talk I could call her any time. I wasn't planning to. I checked out an Alopecia UK Facebook group and felt sorry for a little five-year-old with less hair than me, so cute. But it didn't stop me feeling sorry for myself.

And it bugged me that Daisy didn't. I told Mum her smile got on my nerves. I even hated the way she didn't mind being snubbed by me and wouldn't take offence.

So at first I spun away like a magnet that repels instead of attracting. And Daisy's bareheaded choice made me want a great wig.

Sept 25th

There's a reason why most people with Alopecia cover up. It's too hard without a disguise. I can't wait for the wigs Mum ordered to arrive. I might look human again.

****
****

Mum was driving when I did my hairpiece U-turn. She reminded me that I'd mocked the acrylic one that sat on Frances, and called it a *dead guinea pig.*

"It'd have to be a good one," I said.

"You don't think it's less trouble to go without, like Daisy?"

"Some people don't mind looking like Martians," I said. "I do."

Mum had found out the cost of really convincing ones made of real hair and it was what she called prohibitive. I told her she was starting to talk like Val but she ignored me. "I don't think I can afford it, love, unless we sell the car."

"Sell the car?" I repeated, looking possessively at the shabby interior. It was a mess: crumbs, worn patches, stains on the seats from drink spills. "How would I get anywhere?"

Mum did mention buses but we both knew a deluxe wig costs a lot more than the Old Banger would fetch.

"What am I supposed to do?" I asked.

When we arrived back home she showed me some photos of wigs she'd found online but there was nothing that reminded me of me, my old self.

"That one's pretty," she said, cursor on it.

"You don't believe in being pretty," I reminded her.

She ordered a few in the end, on sale or return.

Sept 28th

Might as well have tried the Pound Shop.

I've gone for the blonde but the flicks make me sick and when you pull them down the hair is too long. I won't be fooling anyone. The sheen's all wrong.

"It looks nice," said Mum. She reckons I didn't give it a chance and anyway people don't inspect anyone with a microscope. Yeah right. Was she never a teenager? Doesn't she know Dee AT ALL?

I've just stuck Nancy on a stand Mum bought me. I call it Nancy because it doesn't look like me. I prefer my French hat after all. Even with a jellyfish edge of trailing hair hanging down underneath. It's thin but it's mine.

I missed my chance with Granny Sylvie and her money. I'm so *stupide*.

****

****

Oct 5th

I caught a stomach bug. Seriously. Mum smelt the sick for herself. I've already had five days off school. My Alopecia's on a roll but I've been too green and grey and empty to count the hairs I've got left.

****
****

Oct 6th

Job done. Totalis. Coot. Huron warrior without the scary ridge on top. Boiled egg, all the shell peeled away. Invader from another galaxy. Weirdo.

All over now.

****
****

When I read that diary entry I remember it exactly. The day I was going back to school (again) the shower captured the last of my hair. In fact there were nine tough individuals hanging on – but at risk. Like all those species on Daisy's Facebook wall.

Mum had already gone off to work. My howl never picked up much volume. Then I decided. To spot those nine hairs randomly scattered around my head anyone would need to invade my space. And that was a chance no one was likely to get. Shaking, I grabbed my nail scissors and sliced each one off, right at the point of exit.

It didn't feel like the start of anything. I'd been on my way to this moment for four months, and give or take a few crazy moments, mainly with Granny Sylvie, I always knew I couldn't sidestep it. But now I felt I needed more time to prepare. Or a way out. Even with exams they let you do a re-sit and sometimes you get a different outcome.

There are things I could have said to myself, like:

It's only hair. Worse things happen. And even: *You're stronger than you think you are.* But I wouldn't have believed me. *Don't be pathetic* would have been good advice to self. But self would probably have hit back with swear words broken up with tears. *I'm allowed,* I thought. So I sobbed.

But no one can cry non-stop. I spent whole long chunks of time in my room, with my eyes closed and almost dry, trying to get lost in music. For two more days I stayed home and begged Mum not to call Dad or contact Daisy. I even kept my phone off. I don't know what I thought I'd achieve by staying in my numb space away from people. Of course Mum said everything you'd expect any mother to say and I turned my head away from most of it. She used words like 'adjust' as if that was as easy as turning up the volume. So I did. I turned the music right up and pretended I couldn't hear her.

Then at the end of the second day she knocked once, barged into my room and said, "Time up, Rowan. You have to live your life."

"I don't know how," I said.

"Then maybe you need to ask Daisy Waterhouse," said Mum.

"I'm not Daisy Waterhouse!" I cried, with a swear word in the middle of her name. "And I don't want to be, all right?"

In that moment I hated Daisy for dealing with something that seemed way too hard for me to bear. And when Mum reminded me that Alopecia wouldn't actually kill me I hated her even more.

"You're kidding!" I cried. "You'll be telling me next the earth isn't flat."

"Well, do you want to give the new wig an airing?"

"I don't *want* to. I don't *want* to leave the house."

My mother nodded slowly, with her mouth tight. "That's why you have to do it," she said.

The words sounded as if she'd chipped them out of stone. I looked at her, with her chin a bit flobby, and the slits in her oversized earlobes heading for the edges after years of heavy metal dangling. My mother: not glamour but granite. Her cheeks were breaking up into specks. I didn't suppose she'd even care if it happened to her. After all, she'd made it clear no man was ever getting near her again.

"Come on," she said. "I'll walk with you."

I told her I wasn't eight. Then I showered and dressed, and tried to train the wig. Nancy sat there on my hot head like a squatter. Or a joke. The flicks were so pert and itchy against my cheek I nearly chopped them. After fifteen minutes of quiet crying I tried to shove my hat on top but it felt jammed and stiff. And when I gave up on that idea, the two came off together and had to be pulled apart.

Mum never stopped the commentary all the way to school. Weren't the flowers lovely? Dodgy weather: BBC said one thing and Yahoo another. She couldn't stand a dog that yapped like that; it went right through her. Was I still reading a book I'd finished months earlier and did I fancy pancakes for supper?

We were seriously late by this time so we hadn't seen anyone in my school uniform, but all the way I kept my eyes ahead – except when there were eyes to avoid. No one laughed or pointed. Some idiot threw a takeaway coffee cup out of the window but no one hurled remarks. At the school gates Mum said she'd come in with me.

"No, I'll be fine."

"You won't do a runner? I don't want to come home and find you back in bed."

I sighed as if she was ridiculous but I managed to thank her.

"You can do it. Decide what you're going to say. Make a joke of it if that's easier."

"A joke?"

"Take control."

"Yes, Mother," I said sarcastically. If I was at the control panel we'd be heading for another galaxy.

"You did text your friends?"

I had: *I'm the one in the crap wig don't laugh.* Probably not the wording Mum had in mind. I hadn't looked at the replies but at that point I checked. *Haha* x That was Dee. At first I didn't know whether it was sick or thick but then it seemed wildly, madly funny. I turned off my phone.

Mum pushed the double doors into Reception and started explaining to the woman on the desk that there was a good reason for me being late. It was the meanest member of the office staff, the one Yasmin called *Bloodhound* because she always sniffed as if she could smell a lie when she heard one. She looked behind Mum at me, peering as if she couldn't recognise me. I was hanging back and trying to keep my eyes on the walls but I felt right under her microscope. Then Mum handed something over and I didn't want to think about what might be in it.

When Mum moved to give me a hug I couldn't let her in case I shrank down to Y2 size. Or decomposed like a corpse, and left nothing behind but the wig lying on the floor, like a mop without the handle. She went off, waving too hard too often. I made my way to the lesson I should be in – only realising as I walked that I'd be making an entrance, like Mum at her clubs. Minus the applause.

Then I remembered her first gig after Dad left, and the way even Zac understood she didn't feel like singing. "Start with *I Will Survive*," I told her. In my head I heard the opening bars and the hurt in Mum's voice the way she sang it in the bathroom. *At first I was afraid, I was petrified.* Outside Set Two English I skipped to the chorus and repeated it as I turned the door handle. Part of me knew, deep down, that the wig was all right – but I wasn't.

Everyone looked up. I didn't try to read the expressions. I was looking at a total stranger, also a man. I flushed.

"Sorry I'm late," I said.

He asked for my name and I nearly said Nancy.

"Whoah," muttered one of the Toms, who does the gardening in the courtyard and gets excited about cabbage. "Quick grow! D'you use fertiliser?"

A few people sniggered but some other boy said, "It's a wig."

"No shit, Sherlock," I said.

And the supply teacher didn't say a word about language. The others laughed and I saw Dee smile. But there was no seat next to her.

I tried not to care that the only space was next to weedy Lucie with hair that smelt overripe, partly because she sucked it. To be honest I'd always tended to ignore Lucie. Now she ignored me.

The supply teacher wanted someone to read and I didn't usually volunteer but this time I knew I could do it. I was acting already and pleased with my performance. As I lost myself in my Oscar-grabbing role I started to have fun. I made everything around me melt away. Daisy would have been proud of me.

After the lesson Dee said, "It suits you."

I wished she hadn't but I touched it like a model in an advert and said, "Thanks. I'm worth it."

When a boy asked if he could try it on I said, "Only if I can try yours," and reached for his head. He escaped, and wiggled down the corridor stroking his (rather lovely) hair.

I laughed as much as anyone. I felt as if I was someone new, someone who just didn't care. The one who scored the final point – and if it was against myself, it counted double.

I must have felt OK when I wrote two pages in my diary.

Oct 14th

Nancy's not so bad for a wig. I think Mum came home expecting to find me in pieces. And in bed. Instead I had the pancake batter mixed all ready. After supper I messaged Daisy to tell her she'd be proud of me.

Yay! she replied. *Remember your track record for getting through tough days is 100% so far. XX*

I pulled a goal back. Alopecia's ahead but I'm closing the gap. X

Alopecia's running scared. You've got it on the ropes, out for the count. XX

Haha I thought you were a pacifist! And rubbish at sport. x

Yeah they're all the same to me. But you won today. Go, Row! XX

No river no boat. I gave that a sad emoticon.

We're in the same one. And I reckon we're afloat. X

Downstairs I overheard Zac asking Mum how come I was suddenly so cocky and she replied, "I think it's Daisy's doing."

Typical. Can you believe it? Don't give me any credit!

Just when I thought we'd finished texting the invitation came: *Dad says you can come to Putney this weekend if you want and meet Flame. He's the boy Mum thinks I'll marry however many times I say we're just best friends.*

So now I'm curious. Knowing Daisy wants to help makes me feel kind of helpless. But I might go. I might even sleep tonight.

****
****

6

I think Zac was glad to get rid of me that Saturday. "I bet Daisy isn't a horrible sister," was what he said.

"She isn't a sister at all!" I cried, hoping she wasn't trying to be mine. "How come you've joined the Fan Club when you've never even met her?"

My friends were impressed by London and a boy called Flame, just the way I meant them to be. But I might not have gone if I'd had other offers. On the surface we were still mates, but they'd been hanging without me while I was off and now I had the feeling they were still doing it, secretly. A whole stack of things had piled up between us, starting with the hat on the coffee shop table. Plus everything I didn't tell them. And what I guessed they said about me.

It was different with Daisy. I can picture her arriving at the station on her bike, in old ripped jeans and a T-shirt that said *Earth Matters*. We must have looked like we didn't belong together. She had a satchel with pigs on it and a Guardian poking out; my bag was big fake D and G and my shoes were out to impress. When the train doors opened she sat down and said she'd save the paper for later. I was focused on being invisible in case anyone around us saw right through Nancy.

"Read it now if you want," I said, and got my phone out.

So we didn't chat that much on the journey, except about films and we'd seen different ones. When she tried to tell me about some old comedy my dad liked too, everything wobbled – earrings, boobs. *OMG embarrassing,* I told Dee by sneaky text. Not mentioning the bare scalp that didn't bother Daisy when she saw it doubled by the carriage window.

Then there was the tube. The young black women opposite us were so fabulous they might have been in a girl band, with long bare legs and perfect eye make-up. One of them had aubergine hair and another had a jet-black swirl piled up on her head with a giant yellow comb. I wasn't fooled by their music. I was sure they knew my secret and I read scorn in their eyes.

They soon got off for shopping but it's a long way round to Putney. We were still a few stops off when a couple of lads got on and grinned as they stood in the gap between us and the American couple opposite. I kept my eyes down and wished I was further from their baggy-jeaned waists. They smelt like customers of Mum's and I knew they'd have the same kind of bellies before long.

"All right, girls?"

As Daisy gave them a quick thumbs-up, it occurred to me that she was giving me away. My wig looked a lot less real next to a bald head. The thought made me redden. The two lads moved further down the carriage but I saw them glance back, sniggering.

"Ignore them," murmured Daisy.

"You girls got far into the treatment?" That was the American mother. Her eyes were full of sympathy as mine looked up, probably wide with horror.

"I finished mine six months ago. All clear." She took off her cap and showed us a short head of white-blonde hair. Her even fatter husband winked at her and smiled at us.

"Cool!" said Daisy, "but ours is Alopecia. It's an auto-immune condition, not an illness. You look really well."

My eyes were burning now. Ours! I was so angry. What gave her the right?

The woman leaned over and said in a kind of stage whisper, "So do you, girls. And you are! But it must be tough all the same. Alopecia! Well you're very brave."

Her husband was nodding and murmuring agreement. She'd been looking at Daisy but then she switched to me.

"It looks great, really, honey. You both look great. I wish you all the best, I really do."

"Thanks," said Daisy. "You too."

I sat dumbly while she asked them where they'd been in London, and where they were heading. The tear I could feel in my eye hadn't gone anywhere so I brushed it with the side of my forefinger and hated the husband for noticing it. As I heard my name with Daisy's I didn't think I'd ever felt so exposed.

Then when the lads got off I heard the word Alopecia said like a joke. The one with a tattoo on the back of his neck glanced back at me as the two of them swaggered away. Two stops later the Americans got off, wishing us a lovely weekend. Daisy squished up her face.

"Sorry. Is that the first time you've had the cancer thing?"

I sniffed.

"It makes you feel guilty in a way, doesn't it?" she continued.

"No."

"It must be amazing to recover like that, when you've had such a shock and been so afraid. They're really happy."

She must have known I wasn't. I felt as if Mum had wasted money she couldn't afford on a wig that was meant to help me cope in the outside world. Being with Daisy Waterhouse blew my cover.

"Here we are," she said. "Putney Bridge."

When Daisy talked about her dad, Steve, I only thought missing fathers were the only other thing we had in common on top of missing hair. I didn't pay attention to the stuff about Flame because I imagined him tall and skinny with glasses and pimply skin.

Flame: just one more thing I was wrong about. The diary for that Saturday says it all. I've even drawn a border of fire around the page, but I could have rained Cupid's arrows everywhere. And I did add a heart at the end.

Oct 16th

OMG I think I'm in love.

****
****

So much has happened since, but that doesn't mean it wasn't huge and real. The day is still vivid, even now.

As we walked to her dad's, Daisy told me a story about a whale in the Thames. She made Flame out to be some kind of wildlife expert because he'd been the first to identify the species. Daisy's the only girl I know who can use the word *sperm* without a smirk.

Then I remembered the TV coverage and how Mum followed it. She can be quite soft on animals for someone who earns her living cooking dead ones – as I told her at the time.

"That was you?" I asked, incredulous.

"All of us, both dads, a whole team with incredible equipment…" The way she told it, I thought Spielberg should be chasing the movie rights. "Flame's going to study Disaster Management at uni," she told me.

Looking at her scalp I could have made a joke about the obvious disaster he couldn't manage. I remembered that Flame was two years older than her so he'd be finishing with school before long.

"Hasn't he got a girlfriend?" I asked.

"There have been a couple but I don't think he's got time, with all the campaigning on top of A Levels."

I thought I knew what that meant: too geeky, spotty, speccy and nerdy to pull anyone. So I wasn't excited at the end of too many stairs up a big old terrace, until a door opened even before she could knock.

Holding it was a tall boy with enough hair for all three of us and smelling of coconut. I took him in, every detail. Long gleaming dreadlocks pulled back from a milky brown forehead. A loose red waistcoat over a yellow T-shirt. Biceps. Loose shorts and long legs. Bare feet on a doormat that said NAMASTE.

The eyes that looked at me (and Daisy) were big and brown. I hope I didn't look the way I felt because that was awestruck, gobsmacked and mesmerised. He was beautiful. Still is.

He gave Daisy a hug and the two of them held on just that extra moment or two that means something more. Beside him she looked smaller, rosier and more freckled than usual. Curvier too, because he was all muscle and bone. The message across his chest said *Way of the Bodhisattvas*. Some cool band, I thought.

"Flame, meet Rowan," she told him as she broke away but stayed close.

"Hey," he said. "Good to meet you, Rowan."

How many seconds did it take, for the runaway feelings to hit the brakes? Not many. Reality made a comeback, highlighting a basic fact. I wasn't the old Rowan Figg: a quite-nice-looking blonde with a wispy teen body. That was the past. I was a girl with no hair and a cheap wig.

And I swear that was the moment when my fit little body lost the ability to hold itself upright, never mind pose. Collapsing on the inside is less dramatic than crashing to the floor and some people may not even see it happening. But I wasn't solid now. I might as well have been some kind of cobweb caught in the doorway.

Then I was being welcomed by his dad, Kyle, hair first. His was pulled flat in a million skinny plaits on top, and then bound where it swelled by rainbow threads of wool. Daisy had said he was the spit of a famous poet I hadn't heard of, but to me he looked like he should be playing guitar on an island with his big brown feet in clear water.

He said Daisy's dad was delayed on a job. I couldn't latch on to all the talk. I was trying to remember stuff I hadn't listened to while I was using my phone. Like Flame having a mum in Sweden? Finland? Being seasick every time he went to stay? And a brother called Red? No, Blue!

Daisy tried hard to include me. "Rowan's mum's a singer," she said, as Flame moved a laptop from the sofa and shut off some bluesy music.

I sat where it had been, on a wrinkled woven throw. "Not like a real one," I said, and then flushed.

"Virtual?" asked Flame, with a smile that melted me.

"Not famous," I said. "She does tatty old clubs and pubs, sixtieth birthday parties…"

"Cool," said Flame.

"You haven't heard her," I muttered.

"I'd like to," he said.

"That takes some spirit," said Kyle, back at the hob.

Yeah, I thought, my mum had all the spirit and I had none. I suppose that was why I put her down the moment I stepped through the door. I realised there was nothing interesting Daisy could say about me, except the obvious fact that was staring everyone in the face. The bald fact.

"So how's it going?" asked Flame.

It? Hair loss? The day? Life? Looking at him? "All right,"
I said.

"No one bats an eyelid in London," he said. "Purple hair,
pink hair, green, none. Burka, turban, kippah."

"Even dreadlocks," said Daisy.

Flame grinned and his swung. So, I thought, it's a double
act. One starts and the other finishes.

"Has anyone given you a hard time, Rowan?" asked Kyle.
"Out in the sticks?"

They were all looking at me.

"I don't go out without a wig," I said. "I don't want to be
stared at. Not like that."

That was when Flame said something about people in cities
feeling like cogs in something that didn't work and Daisy said
maybe they'd lost more than hair. It was when I knew I didn't
speak the same language as the rest.

And I could smell things I'd never eaten. Panicking, I
wondered whether they might pray to some god or other before
they picked up the cutlery. Or invite some smelly homeless
people in to share the meal. Right on cue, so Kyle could serve
up, Flame tidied the *Big Issue* from the wooden, picnic-type
table with benches round it.

"Seen this one, Daise?" he asked her.

She said there was a great piece about female role models
but I didn't recognise any names. Including someone called
Polly who had been missed out, so they'd both tweeted the
magazine. Or retweeted each other. They must have expected
me to ask who she was, but I didn't want them to tell me
together, finishing each other's sentences. Then Kyle tried to

pass the mic back to me. I was studying the food on my plate trying not to look panicked.

"D'you have a role model, Rowan?" he asked.

Some pop star that makes headlines by being outrageous? That would have been Dee's answer and it's kind of rebellious but predictable at the same time. A sexy, powerful woman with great, expensive clothes and six inch heels.

I looked around. It was the only answer I had and it wouldn't fit. But Flame's brown eyes were on me and the heat was up again under my cheeks. My wig pricked.

"I don't know," I said. In school that answer's standard. But now it felt pathetic.

Flame bailed me out by telling me his mum was his hero. He said she'd once helped to wreck a war plane in a hangar so it couldn't bomb anyone, and got off all charges because the judge agreed she'd only broken the law to prevent a more serious crime. Those eyes of his were big and shiny with pride but it didn't seem the kind of thing mothers did, or should do. Dee's did manicures and Yasmin's mum made cushions.

Then it was time to eat. And time for me to come across like a child, a fusspot, a junk food addict and an anorexic – as well as the only carnivore. There was no coke and the bread had seeds. I poked something Daisy said was okra.

"Oprah Winfrey," I blurted suddenly. "She's a role model. I mean, she started off with nothing and look at her now, one of the richest women in America. She gave cars away on one show – did you see? These women were all screaming. My mum wished she'd been in that audience. Our car's junk."

Maybe I imagined the silence.

"She started her book club," said Daisy, "because books gave her hope when she needed some."

I hadn't thought of that. I'm not sure I knew. They all talked books as they ate and I poked my food about. Then there was a ring on the doorbell.

It was Daisy's dad, Steve Waterhouse, smelling of orange blossom and greeting Daisy with an "All right, Twinkletoes?" He had gelled, glossy hair and a smile that was cute for his age. "You must be the lovely Rowan!" he cried, and I thought, I used to be. "Any chance you can keep Daise under control? This lot are no help. They'll have you on some demo if you're not careful."

He was clean and chirpy. I couldn't help thinking that if Mum wanted the house decorated he'd be first choice. And the place would fill with banter.

"I should know," he said. "They got me at it. FRACK OFF and all that." He leaned towards me. "MI6 probably have this place bugged. HQ for the revolution."

"The Great Turning," said Daisy.

"See? Give them half a chance and they'll turn you!"

He sat down to eat and suddenly Daisy asked me if I liked dance, as if it was a big deal.

"Sure," I said. "I can throw some shapes. I did tap and modern for years, three merits, four distinctions." I wasn't sure I'd pulled that bragging off. "I really fancy the tango."

I had a partner in mind and it wasn't Daisy, even though she jerked her head like a pro and set off across the room with an arm straight ahead like a spear and a look that was meant to smoulder until it cracked into a laugh.

Flame said she was in a primary school production as the White Witch. The way she looked up when he called her performance 'awesome', I was sure she was in love with him. Kyle asked me about reggae and next thing I knew Daisy and Flame were moving to Bob Marley in some routine that was half cool and half a mess because they hadn't tried it for years, and Daisy kept laughing at Flame getting the sequence wrong. He looked good to me. I could have watched him all night.

When the sun came shining in, Flame suggested a walk near Putney Bridge. The wind felt Siberian and my shoes had finally managed to tear skin at the back of both heels, but between Flame and Daisy was a good place to be. They named flowers, arguing once or twice, teasing. But I don't mean they ignored me. They were like a couple with a house to sell, wanting to show me around. But it would have taken one of those whales they'd saved to take my mind off my blisters and rattling teeth.

I was too busy fiddling with Nancy's flyaway strands to notice the branch until it hooked me – by my wig! I felt it tugged, yanked across and up to one side. Not right off but hardly on either. It was caught like a nest some bird had kicked out. The noise I made was half gasp, half scream. I took root, terrified that if I reached for it the branch would swing away and snatch the whole thing. And catapult it into the Thames.

Flame was quicker than Daisy – and a lot quicker than me. Still only my mouth moved at all. Flame's tall enough for basketball so he didn't even have to stretch. Without one word he just unhooked it, while Daisy told me it was all right and put a hand on my arm to stop me shaking. My hands shot out to settle the thing down again before it could slip to the ground the second he freed it.

"Thanks," I said. But part of me wished it had been anyone but him.

The incident's not there in my diary and it's quite a big OMG to leave out. A choice. I wanted to think about Flame and just Flame, without that memory of him touching me/not-me/Nancy. Of course I told myself it could have been worse. And I suppose if that branch had robbed me of the whole wig, leaving me bareheaded in front of him, he might have had to fish me out of the river.

Even as it was, I couldn't stop shivering even after we turned back – not to Flame's but Steve's flat above. We were off to a dance show, the three of us, and it was Daisy's surprise so I tried not to look what Mum called sullen.

Hugs all round. I didn't time the big one between Flame and Daisy but I was sure it was the longest. I was one step back, conscious of the boobs in my uplift bra that would feel a lot bigger pressed against his chest. But he kissed me on each cheek, like my French step-mum. I felt a dreadlock brush against my neck in passing, quick and light but lovely. I told myself he wanted me to know it was all right now: everything.

No offence to Daisy but after that nothing else made the same impression. The dance show was hip-hop, and Dee and Yasmin would have been jealous as well as impressed, but it's hard to compete with a kiss from a dreadlocked god – or a wig on a branch.

I did like the show. But Daisy couldn't wait to get back to Putney to do her own take on some of the moves. I mean literally couldn't wait, starting on the tube platform. If I'd sent a text I would have said she was *OMG so embarrassing* but she was good, crazy good. Steve wasn't.

Steve Waterhouse's place is neat like him, always just-painted and very male – apart from Daisy's room, which has dark red walls and prints in clip-frames of Victorian girls with big hair. I didn't sleep much. You can't plan your dreams and mine was more of a nightmare about a fat pigeon laying eggs in a blonde nest with upward flicks. I slept in on the Sunday and by the end of the morning we were heading back for the train. No goodbyes at the downstairs flat because Flame and Kyle were out, on some kind of training.

I didn't find out what that meant because my phone rang on the street not far from the tube.

"Hello," said a familiar voice. "Who's this I'm calling?"

"Sylvie!" I cried, shouting because of the traffic.

"Another Sylvie? In England? Sylvie who?"

I giggled. "No, Granny Sylvie, this is Rowan."

"Rowing? A boat?"

"Rowan," I yelled, as it suddenly stopped being funny. "Your granddaughter."

"Rowan," she said. "You're losing your hair!"

"No," I told her, "I lost it. It's gone."

"Come over! I know a trichologist in Paris."

I found myself pulling a face at Daisy even though I didn't know what she might have heard. "We went, Granny," I said. She was silent on the end of the phone. Music blared from a smoker's car window. "Sylvie?" I shouted.

"Who is this?" was the last thing I heard. Then a bus went past and I saw *Call Ended.* I clamped my mouth tight, lips pulled right in so that nothing wobbled out.

"Are you all right?" asked Daisy, with a voice that meant she knew I wasn't.

"She was fine in August," I said, "just a bit crazy."

Daisy put an arm round me and I cried.

Oct 17th

How can things change so fast? Granny Sylvie's mind is full of holes! I yelled at Dad to do something. He says she's hard to get hold of and she forgets to return his calls. Maybe she's forgotten who he is but he's not allowed to forget her.

I'd like to forget I've got Alopecia. Or maybe I want everyone else to forget. That's the point of wigs but there's no point in Mum robbing a bank now because the best in the world won't fool anyone.

I'm back home and suddenly Zac's best mates with Dario. Everything feels weird and London seems like a movie now. With a gorgeous lead but the wrong girl cast opposite him. If I was the scriptwriter I'd kill her off.

Flame. I've just been losing myself on his Facebook wall.

Rowan and Flame: destiny. If he likes Daisy so much with zero hair and a bigger bum he could LOVE me, couldn't he? It's not impossible.

I don't know if I'm happy or really REALLY sad.

7

Mum pointed out that Granny Sylvie had been a bit strange for years. As she kept on cutting bread I accused her of not listening and not caring about her own mother-in-law because she was 'jealous'. Maybe the j word was a link.

"So what was Flame like?" she asked, two slices later.

I scowled a moment but it was one change of subject I couldn't resist. "All right," I said. "He's nice. So's his dad. He liked the sound of you!"

"He can like away," she said. "As far as men are concerned, I'm done."

I'd heard it all before. What I'd never understood was why my parents got together in the first place. It wasn't as if they had some uber-obvious bond like Flame and Daisy, who acted like they'd got joint membership of everything. Then I remembered I had photos to show Mum on my phone. At the sight of Flame she raised her eyebrows and then winked. I glared, snatched my phone away and told her, "You're SO annoying and SO unbelievably thick!"

Later she came knocking on my door. "Rowan, I just checked your timetable. You do know it's swimming tomorrow?"

I swore and she didn't react. She just came in and sat on the end of the bed where I lay listening to music. I didn't turn off and I kept my eyes on the wall.

"What do you want to do?" she shouted, as if we were in a stadium and one of her favourite heavy metal bands was playing. "About SWIMMING?"

I cut my own music. "I'll just pull off my wig and jump in," I said, "nice and streamlined. If some bored lad steals it to prance around like a drag queen and get a laugh, I'm sure I'll find him in the end. I can always rescue it if it's blocking a loo in the boys' toilets."

Mum frowned at me. "Funny," she said. "You have lockers, with keys?"

"What's the point of wearing a wig if I'm just going to take it off and let everyone SEE?"

"You could wear a swimming cap. Maybe I can get on Facebook and borrow you one in time."

I stared as if she'd lost the plot, because I thought she had. "That'd be the same thing! It'd be so OBVIOUS and so UGLY!"

"You know you can't stay off…"

"Write me a note, then. Say I can't swim for emotional reasons. Or I'll have to have my period for the next seven Mondays."

Mum was giving the forefinger a rest but I didn't kid myself she'd given up. At bedtime she said she knew I wouldn't let swimming set me back.

"No way," I said.

The next morning I came downstairs to find my nicest swimming costume wrapped in a towel inside my sports bag. So I slung it over my shoulder, marched into the kitchen and unzipped it in front of her. Then I dumped the contents on the tiles with the crumbs from Zac's toast. His mouth would have sprung open if it hadn't been full.

"You forgot the shampoo," I said.

I took a piece of toast from Zac's plate and left with a bang of the front door. I heard her call my name three or four times but I didn't look round and she wasn't in any shape to catch me.

On the bus the back seat was taken, and where I sat there were some Y7 boys behind me, close enough to touch. The ride felt like an hour and even though I held myself firm and stiff, every time one of them giggled I burned. As the bus drew closer to school I needed help from someone who understood. Or used to. Because I knew she'd never do what I was doing. Maybe that's why I had to do it.

Daisy it's swimming, I said, *any ideas?X*

I know you won't believe me just yet but that's lovely without hair, she said. *But I'm sure school can lend you a hat. Tough it out either way. It'll help. And when the rest look all bedraggled afterwards you'll be perfect XX.*

What did I expect, I thought, from Little Miss Sunshine and her solar panels?

You can do it, she added. *Alopecia will be heading for relegation. X*

I can't, I told her, but before I could switch off she was back:

You can. Fat kids have to. X

I thought of Judith Hebbon. Her five-foot-ten body got squeezed out where it should be in, round the middle, but was so flat higher up that people said she never wore a bra. I thought of a boy in Y7 who only bared his chins in class but would have to flob around the pool like a walrus. I used to look at people like that as if they were bad smells. Now I was one of them.

I'm not like you, I sent. Then I thought she'd think I meant she was fat too, which she wasn't, only solid. But Daisy never thinks like that.

You don't have to be, she replied. *You can be yourself. It's OK. Walk tall. Take their breath away. XX*

Her clapping emoticon didn't work any magic. When the rest of the class headed off to the pool I managed to slip off to the library, with a finger to my lips for Dee as I turned the other way down the corridor. The LRC has a few armchairs that can hide someone my size from behind. And no one suspects people who are busy reading or taking notes. I managed to get some homework done and I admit I felt a kind of buzz. The thrill of beating the system.

Only it turns out the system is what they call more 'robust' than that. As soon as morning break began I made my way to the toilets. I heard familiar voices as a group of girls from my year burst in.

"She might be in here," said someone.

"Farrow's calling her mum at the burger van."

"You don't think she's... you know... like...?"

"Topped herself?"

I sat there, anxiety going into overdrive at the thought of what I'd started and Mum having the same thoughts.

"I would if I was her!" I heard. "Oh my god! I'd slit my throat!"

I was so angry. I didn't reason that I couldn't stay in that cubicle all day – or as long as it took for the firemen to arrive. It was rage that did it. I pulled the bolt and stepped out. But I didn't slap their faces. I just strolled across to the wash basins without looking at them, as if they weren't even there.

"You wouldn't," I said, casually. "Suicide's overkill." I dried my hands without checking in the mirror. I didn't want to see their faces or mine.

"I meant you're really brave," said one, her voice all cloying and sticky-sweet.

A couple of others agreed. I almost laughed.

"That's the last thing I am," I said. "Brave is when you know you're sick or dying and you live your life the best you can anyway."

That might sound strong on the page (and very Daisy) but my voice was so shaky it almost rattled. It silenced them anyway, until I heard as I walked out, "They're looking for you!"

"Is that right?" I called back. In my head Granny Sylvie said, *"Magnifique"*, but I had a feeling no one else was going to agree.

I reported to Reception and nearly cried when I saw big, cuddly Mrs O'Reilly behind the desk. Bloodhound and Co always look at us as if we're extra-large nits ready to jump and take up residence unless they zap us. But Mrs O really seems to like us.

"Oh, Rowan," she said, "are you all right, love? They've been hunting for you everywhere." She told me to sit down on the visitors' sofa and sent for a glass of water. "I'll call off the sniffer dogs," she whispered, and smiled.

But the sniffer dogs came as a pack, barking quietly to each other as they advanced down the corridor.

"I've been a lot of trouble," I said, before they could decide who spoke first: the head of year, Deputy Head, swimming teacher or Inco. I can't complain – they were nice in a careful way, as if we were all at a funeral. Obviously they thought what I did was a cry for help, and I was fragile and needed more support. So I had to stop them before there was a policy.

"I won't do it again," I said.

Then just as I hoped I could go back to lessons and pretend nothing had happened, there was Mum, rumbling across the car park towards the magic doors in her apron and little hat.

"She forgot her frying pan," I said.

Mrs O was the only one who enjoyed the joke. The "*Sorry*" I mouthed at Mum didn't stop her head shaking at me. No hug. The Deputy Head whisked us all off to his office and I wondered whether any of them would notice if I just hung back and let them walk ahead without me.

No one seemed to realise it was over. I'd gone as far as I dared and crossed my own line, which isn't comfortable. I was back behind it now.

All a bit extreme, I sent to Daisy. *Been there now done that got the T-shirt. X*

You sound stronger for it, she said. *XX*

For my hissy fit? I think I might be. X

You are, she said. *I know you are. XXX*

That's Daisy for you.

Oct 20th

I just wrote Granny Sylvie a proper snail mail letter, with photos to help her work out who I am. And I told Dad to try harder. Things you don't like and can't deal with don't just vanish in a puff of smoke if you ignore them. I should know.

Today I friended two of Daisy's friends on Facebook. Jess is in Australia and looks great with masses of curly hair so she can stay there. But I'm going to meet Nina soon. She's Polish and very skinny. Her English is good, better than Dee's!

My old friends are acting as if we're OK so I suppose we are. Except that's what we're doing, all of us – acting.

Daisy's lent me a book she calls inspiring but I haven't opened it. It's not a novel. It's about the state of the world. Do I have to? Don't think so.

****
****

Oct 21st

Found out who Polly is. Some top barrister who wants Ecocide to be a crime. Daisy thinks they'll pass a new law at the United Nations in 2020 and that'll save the earth and all the ecosystems. Which will save us too.

Yeah right.

Is that what *naïve* means? I looked it up. *Lacking experience, wisdom or judgement.* I can't tick that. If Daisy lacks that lot where am I? But when people say someone's naïve they mean the things they believe in won't happen until hell freezes over. That's what Mum thinks. People will always make a mess of things so that's bound to include the planet. So much for that spirit she's meant to have.

Think I've got a bit more of that myself. Flame texts me now. Just checking how I am and what I've been up to but my heart jumps every time I see his name. I really compose mine, and delete a lot. He must like me? Maybe I've been hard on Nancy and I'm still pretty.

Yeah right. Who's being naïve now? As in *dreaming, out of it.*

Hope Sylvie writes back.

****
****

Oct 26th

Half Term. Yasmin's flying off to the sun but I'm not jealous. I'd hate to wear a wig in real heat. God knows what I'm going to do in France next summer. Dee has gone to Ireland for her uncle's funeral but she says they know how to party. Granny Sylvie could be dead too for all anyone knows.

I might sleep for Britain if I get the chance. I've got way too much work but Daisy says exams are overrated and human beings are more than grades. Mum doesn't like the sound of that.

Hehe. It'd be funny if she thought St Daisy was a bad influence.

****
****

Oct 28th

Does Daisy Waterhouse have any normal friends? I don't mind Nina being Polish or having a weird kind of great voice but she played something she's written herself and it's a love song! She wouldn't tell and blushed. OMG she'd better not know Flame better than I do! And tomorrow she's rock climbing! I couldn't believe it. She's the size of a ten-year-old.

If she was on a real rock instead of a fibreglass copy, the first wind would blow her right off.

Nothing from Dee. Must be too drunk to text.

Nothing from Sylvie either. *Rien.*

****
****

It was just a visit to Nina. We spent most of that day at Daisy's house, with lots of flower prints around the place and a little garden full of the real thing. Molly Waterhouse is a softie. I could feel it in the way she welcomed me with a hug. Daisy showed me the ruined castle which is mainly just space, and we walked by the canal. When she said she'd have to get her phone out for a photo, I thought she meant me, so I did the celebrity hands-over-face plus swear word. But she meant the water. It was reflecting autumn leaves.

Then we took the bus to Nina's. It's cheap and run-down where she lives, with more rubbish. Going up to her flat you see notices everywhere, telling people the area under the stairs isn't for storage when it's jam-packed with bikes, skateboards, boxes and push-along toys. And *NO SMOKING* either but the worn carpet on the stairs stinks of fags. The doors look thin enough to be pushed in by a couple of cops.

I remember Nina's mum was out cleaning and I thought Nina might have had rubber gloves on too because the flat smelt like a hospital.

I'd never met anyone so polite. She'd cooked us a Polish dish and I probed it suspiciously. Not being so polite myself.

"Daisy saved my life," she said. That was about the boy who bullied her in Y6 until he switched targets, leaving the Polish girl alone to focus on the bald one. She smiled at Daisy, who said she'd survived. I didn't mind Nina until she fetched an old guitar and proved what Daisy had said about her singing. Not with Mum's volume but a kind of eerie sadness. She smiled very coyly when it came to the love song.

I tried to quiz Daisy but if she knew Nina was as obsessed with Flame as I was, she wasn't letting on.

Oct 30th

Words won't do it. I don't know what to write. Why me? How can I party with Flame (and Daisy and Nina) when my mother's a lesbian in love with Val next-door?

8

Lads like Aaron used 'gay' to mean uncool, geeky and all those other things they reckon they're not. But I thought I was cool with LGBT. I had no problem with anyone being in a same-sex relationship. Except my mother.

And scatty, straggly, superior Val, who had got on my nerves from the start. If she was talking when I appeared in my own house she just carried on. Maybe she knew I gave Mum a hard time but I thought her Dario was the brat. I didn't know or care what her part-time job was but it seemed to earn her a lot more money than Mum's two. She had an extension, a brand new people carrier and old stuff she called antiques. And her enormous rabbit, Pure, was allowed inside when it was cold so it could leave white hairs and black pellets behind. I didn't trust Val's sandwiches.

That Saturday afternoon my mood was already dark because I'd been stood up outside River Island by some not-so-close friend. I knew *Oops forgot* meant she'd had a better offer than the sad girl in a wig.

So I was back in the kitchen forty-five minutes after I left, ready to sound off to Mum. But she wasn't there. The thudding of a football against Val's wall made me look out of the kitchen window and spot the two of them on our garden seat. They were in a patch of sun, where they could hear the boys on the other side of the fence, and call out over it. But hidden from view.

They sat holding hands. Then Val stroked Mum's neck and I clutched the worktop as they kissed. Not a lunge or a snog but the kind of little kiss old married couples share when they pucker up. It's not so sweet or innocent when it's your mother and the woman next-door.

I'm not proud now but I gave Mum hell. Starting with a bang on the window just so they'd know I was there. Their hands separated and Mum stood, slowly, but it was Val who gave me a friendly smile. Mum asked me what happened and if I was all right. I shook my head fiercely, shut the kitchen door hard and raced upstairs, my chest heaving and caving. But in seconds I heard Mum downstairs. I stared in the bathroom mirror at the bald girl with the lesbian mother. I pictured the school corridors, heard them. Then I saw my glossed lips set tight. It was Mum's mouth when someone's gone too far. And she had.

Below I heard Zac, whining – because she'd stopped the game, and because Dario should be sent off. I stomped down and found him sulking in the kitchen, holding the scissors and looking for some red card to chop up and show Dario.

"What do we have to talk about?" he wanted to know. "I hate talking!"

I made an entrance. Mum looked at me, head on, steady.

"I'm sorry you found out like that, love," she said. As if a brisk enough voice can brush anything away. "You've had enough to deal with." She turned to Zac, who had the bits-and-bobs drawer out on the tiles and was rummaging like a burglar. "Me and Val, we're a couple. We're in love."

My brother looked as if someone had just tried to explain nuclear physics.

"So you're a LIAR?" I demanded, refusing to sit down. "You've been lying to me all my life."

"And myself, Rowan," she said. She told Zac to sit down.

"But maybe it's a PHASE?" I yelled. "You know, you're angry, and on the rebound?"

"I'm not," she said, "It's who I am, always have been." She looked at the string, envelopes and tape my brother had spilt on the tiles. "Zac, there's no red card, all right? Trust me!"

I stared at her. "We can't trust you, though! I don't even KNOW you!"

But she just clenched, mouth tight, and helped Zac clear his mess away. What did he want for tea? Fried egg and sausage. The pair of them just dropped into routine, like that song, *Back to Life, Back to Reality.* But I felt like my reality was over. It was like the hair all over again, gone. I didn't know whether to crash upstairs or out, or give her the silent treatment. The usual phubbing couldn't be enough.

I didn't want her cooking for me so I went for the biscuit tin but it was empty. She started talking. While she cooked she told us how our granddad hated 'poofs'. He was ex-army and he thought the Forces should be straights only.

"I fell for a girl at school. Spent all my Saturday wages on a Valentine's card." She shook her head. "She never even invited me to her sixteenth birthday bash, the cow!"

It was more of a chuckle than a laugh but I still couldn't believe it. I knew Daisy would feel sorry for her but that just made me angry instead.

"You should have shacked up with some woman in the first place!" I said, "and spared us the bother of being born."

"I like being born," said Zac and Mum ruffled his hair. Then she looked at me but I told her I didn't want my scalp stroked, thanks. Brushing past her, I dropped two slices of bread in the toaster.

When she started on Dad and what a sham it was, just wishful thinking, I put my music in my ears. It was too much to take in. I didn't even try to lip-read. I just tore bits off dry toast, drank my tea and scrolled down my phone. But part of me wanted to know. So I cut the music and heard the bit about loving Val from the time she arrived next-door but saying nothing because of the husband.

"Couldn't you carry on saying nothing," I asked, "because of us?"

"That's what I've been doing," she said.

"Sneaking around?"

"Being discreet..."

"That's Val's word, not yours! You're talking like her now."

I could see from Mum's mouth that it was locked tight to hold other words back. She opened a can of beans.

"But I'm glad you found out," she said, scraping the tin. "Truth's a lot healthier than lies."

"Who says?" I wanted to know. "Anyway, broccoli's a lot healthier than chips but what do YOU sell?"

Zac asked whether you can deep-fry broccoli – and Dario was his step-brother now.

"You hate Dario!" I said.

"Only sometimes," he said. "Brothers are cool."

That was quite a cue so I told him they're not and I should know. Mum put a plateful in front of me and I was too hungry to make a statement. I just took it into the lounge and ate on my lap.

When I couldn't concentrate on the TV I rang Dad but he didn't sound surprised.

"It's a shock for you," he said, "but does it make a lot of difference, really? Your mum's not fifty yet. You wouldn't want her to be alone for the rest of her life. There was bound to be someone sometime."

He said we'd get used to it and Val was a good woman.

"What's good about her?" I asked. "Not her housekeeping or her figure. She's a rubbish mother too."

Dad has a very quiet sigh but I think I heard it cross the Channel.

"It's Half Term, isn't it? Do you want to come over?"

"Half Term is half over," I said, and he gave up without a fight.

Mum was the fighter and we'd been clashing for years but she knew me deep down and I wanted to know her too. She kept trying to talk but I'd heard more than I could digest as it was.

"I need to get ready soon," she told me. I remembered she was booked to sing at the new wine and coffee bar on Daisy's high street, but I was back on the sofa watching TV. I didn't look round. "But I'd like to talk first," she said, still in the lounge doorway. "I don't want to leave you like this."

"Like what?" I asked.

"Troubled?" she suggested. "Angry? Ashamed? Confused?"

I didn't tick or cross any of those. I didn't know what I was.

"I don't want it to come between us," she said. "You're my best girl, you know that."

I hoped she wasn't going to wink. She came over to the sofa and lifted her arms as if she wanted to take off. Mine just lay there with the remote.

"It's OK," I said. "You get ready."

Sometimes I told her to knock them all dead or make them shut up and listen. I wanted to find something better to say but my mouth set hard. Once her shower started running I turned down the volume on the TV. I listened, for her to start singing the way she usually did before a gig to ease her voice in, but there were no vocals this time.

Flame's text was good timing even if it was a slow reply to a friendly one I'd sent that morning. He asked how my day had been.

Bombshell, I answered, so he rang me. As soon as my phone started ringing I hurried upstairs, heart tight. Lying on the bed, I felt my own breathing, sure it would squeeze my voice if I spoke. It took a while for me to put the words together so he could understand what I meant. As I smoothed the duvet around me, I pictured him sprawled on the sofa with the throw, his knees bent and his brown feet bare.

"Don't get me wrong," I told him, "I'm all for equal rights and that stuff."

"Yeah," he said. "It's all love. And whoever she's with doesn't change how she feels about you."

Trying to remember the last time I'd heard a boy use the L word, I wondered what it would take to make him love me. London seemed a long way away.

"And it doesn't change the way you feel about her." That didn't seem to be a question.

"I just feel like I've lost my mother."

As I spoke I pulled off my wig because my head was overheating. I dropped it on the bed and kicked it over with my foot, like Zac with a can in the gutter.

"Tell me all about her," said Flame. "The times she's stood up for you and made you laugh, or proud, or made things better."

"How long have you got?" I asked, and he chuckled.

"Go on," he said.

So I gave him a splurge. Mum waking us up on Christmas morning with a bluesy *Mary's Boy Child* morphing into *Winter Wonderland*. The embarrassment when she won the Parents' sack race at primary school Sports Day, with the power of a kangaroo and big boobs bouncing. Mum in borrowed overalls, knocking out a fireplace with a sledgehammer, climbing a ladder and painting the whole house after Dad had gone.

103

Charging into the grey sea at Cromer even though her legs were purple-white in the bitter wind, with Zac chasing her laughing, and me yelling, *"You're CRAZY!"* The first time I ever saw her cry, by the bed where my grandpa lay in hospital. *"I wish you knew who I am, Dad,"* she said.

I stopped.

"That's sad," said Flame. "She thought he couldn't accept her as she was."

"So I have to," I mumbled.

"It's what we all need." He sounded so sunny it was hard to feel quite as stormy now. "Daisy expects it: not just acceptance but respect. And she gets it, mostly. Kevin Prices are rare."

"Mm." I remembered the name of the bully who picked on Daisy till she saw him off.

"You have to respect yourself first," he said.

I wondered whether we were talking about Mum again, or Daisy or me. Then he asked me if I wanted to go to a party. "Maybe Daisy's already said?"

"No," I said. "For Hallowe'en?"

"Kind of an alternative. Crazy games, pumpkin pie and candles. No vampires, though."

I checked whether it was religious and he said not in the way I meant but the local Imam would be there as well as a cool vicar he called 'radical'.

"What's *Way of the Bodhisattvas*?" I asked, picturing his chest the first time I saw it.

He told me it was a Buddhist idea and they were *enlightenment beings* showing the way.

"Cool," I said, hoping I didn't sound alarmed. He said Daisy would be in touch.

It crossed my mind that Daisy hadn't mentioned this party because she might not want me there. But it turned out, when she sent a text two minutes later, that Nina was coming too. So not exactly a date.

I picked up the wig and shook it. "Dummy," I muttered.

Just then Mum knocked. She was in brand new singing gear but even though the top was shimmery gold she didn't look very sparkly. I realised her bare arms were getting older as well as thicker.

"You know I'd cancel the gig but they'd never ask me again."

"Sure," I said, and shaped a smile.

"You don't fancy coming?"

"Maybe next time," I said. *But not with Val,* I thought. I looked at the top. "Is that from her?"

"Late birthday present." She didn't ask if I liked it.

"It's not you," I said, as she walked away.

Nov 1st

Nina fancies the hell out of Flame and she has a voice as well as HAIR. It got a bit limp and drippy at the All Saints' Party though. Shame! After she'd curled it too.

Weird party. No masks or fake blood, just lots of tea lights and pumpkin pie. We were meant to remember the dead but I don't know who my ancestors were. Maybe some of them had

Alopecia under their bonnets. Passing the balloon under your chin isn't so stupid when you're behind Flame in the line. Except that Nina was in front of him. The apple bobbing meant *rien* until some woman showed what to do. Face down in the bucket.

So I left. Daisy was straight after me, before Flame got a chance. No one asked her to miss the fun. I can just see her ducking her whole scalp under and nutting the apple up out of the water like a seal with a ball.

"Gets in the way, doesn't it?" she said. Meaning the A word. "Jumps out and hits you without warning."

No kidding, Daisy. My whole life does that to me.

She says we have to be the best ancestors we can be for people of the future, and change the world for them. She goes on about how connected we all are, to other living beings and the trees. It's Flame she wants to connect with but she doesn't know it yet.

Or she's not saying. Like Mum with Val.

****
****

Nov 2nd

OMG Sylvie's here. I think she's come for me. Five rings on the doorbell and there she stood beside her Paris suitcase, waving to a taxi driver. No explanation, just a hug for me, and "Amelie, your poor hair!" Kisses on the cheeks for Zac, but only because she thinks he's Dad. So far she's ignored Mum except for asking a few times who she is.

"Do you clean?" she asked her after supper.

"Not much," said Zac. He tries not to giggle but I don't think Sylvie would notice. It's so sad.

She touched my wig when she went to bed. SO tenderly, I felt choked. I found the red leather hat to jog her memory but she said it wouldn't fit on top of a wig and I shouldn't squash it. Her hair's even longer – not snow-white, more polar bear – but it could do with some Guillaume magic. It makes her look older and paler.

Now Mum's on the phone to France, as if Dad does action! I think she could do without a crazy guest right now. Sausage, mash and onion rings don't really cut it with Sylvie. Nor does a screw-top bottle of what she called, "Plonk?" as if it ends with a q u e. The two of them were never soulmates like me and my granny.

I like it when she calls me *chérie*. It's not all about me and my Alopecia any more, or Mum and Val. But I wish I could have my Paris gran back again.

9

Even now I still want Sylvie back. And we still do the exaggerated "Plonque?" joke every time there's *vin* around, even though Val takes her wine seriously. She's done a course.

Granny Sylvie arrived full of the old Paris energy. But she'd catnap four times a day and then we'd hear her up in the night, turning on the TV or opening cupboard doors. Mum had no idea what to do about her, and Dad didn't seem to be in any rush to come and fetch her. Half Term was over and Mum couldn't let her *Reckless* regulars down, but Val kept an eye on Sylvie and her movements. So we knew she went out each day in a taxi, but when we asked her where she'd been, she only talked about coffee and cake, dogs and the weather.

Mum rang the taxi firm. Sylvie had booked the same driver for the same time each day, and asked him to call her when he was on the way so she didn't forget. She said she'd 'go crazy' if she stayed indoors on her own. Cue splutter from Zac.

The driver's instructions were to take her to interesting places and be back by half-past three (when 'Amelie' came home from school). If Zac had football or some other club we'd be on our own again, Sylvie and me.

"We have to look after you, chérie," she'd say, and, "You're too precious to lose."

Normally I hated being questioned but I could tell Sylvie anything. It felt so safe. She didn't really talk to Mum or Zac and she forgot most of it anyway. So I told her I was mad about a boy and showed her Flame's picture on Facebook. I even removed my wig and let her massage my scalp while I watched TV. But it set her off talking about hospital, treatment and being sick.

"I'm not sick," I told her. "Only of Alopecia, anyway."

She got it for a while but before long I was Amelie again and I started to get the feeling she was mourning me before I'd died.

Dad had never told Mum the details of what happened to his little sister. And I think Mum was having enough trouble in the present without investigating the past. I glared at her whenever she tried talking to Sylvie about going back to France.

"I can't leave my girl," Sylvie said, next to me at the supper table. She set her chips aside and smiled just for me. "She needs me."

Mum's eyes told me to say I'd be fine but I didn't want Sylvie to go.

"Your poor hair," she said, in that wistful way, and patted my wig. Zac was never allowed within arm's reach of Nancy, but Sylvie was so careful and fond. "I'm so sorry, chérie. I'll stay to the end."

"The end of what?" asked Zac, but Sylvie didn't explain. "When's Dad coming?"

"Bless you," she said. "I left him. Love can be cruel. We'll send for him when the time comes."

"What time?" pushed Zac.

"Oh, about time I expect," said Sylvie, and laughed the way she had in the car on the French motorways when she sang to jazz. "It's *le weekend* tomorrow so we must have some fun."

That sounded all right to me. Daisy was supposed to be coming over on the bus but I cancelled her. Maybe I was afraid Sylvie would see her bare head, call her Amelie and stroke her instead. Zac said he was playing football but Sylvie wanted to take me shopping and I wasn't going to object to that. But she fell asleep on the sofa with her head forward and her mouth open, so when the phone rang I ran to answer because Mum was out singing.

It was Dad. He said he was coming to take Sylvie back.

"She's all right here," I said. "She shouldn't be on her own."

"I've told her she can live with us but all she talks about is taking care of Amelie."

I guessed that must be hurtful for Dad, being ignored or forgotten.

"We can take care of each other," I said.

"Amelie died, Rowan…"

"I know!"

"When she was your age, more or less exactly."

"Do you even know my age?" I asked. I don't know why I was giving him such a hard time but I was shaken.

"In any case," he said, "she's my responsibility."

"But she doesn't want to be anyone's responsibility," I told him. "No one does. She wants to be needed and I need her."

At Dad's end I imagined a faint sigh. "Tell Mum I'll see you about three."

"All right," I said, "but you might need handcuffs. She won't want to go, not without me."

He could have carried her over his shoulder. Really I knew my parents were right about why she should leave. She was French, Dad was her next of kin and she had a house I just about remembered that couldn't be left to rot. I guessed she needed medical help for whatever the French called dementia. And she was a liability. But I couldn't see that any of that mattered as much as what she wanted: to be with me.

"She'll get harder to manage," Dad said. "You think she's funny now…"

"I love her!" I said. I loved her for loving me even though she thought I was someone else. Remembering she was asleep on the sofa, I lowered my voice and said I'd see him tomorrow. I couldn't wake her, even for shopping.

I found Sylvie doing warm-up exercises, leaning slowly over and stretching.

"Bedtime, chérie," she told me. "You should keep your strength up. Do you remember when I used to sing you to sleep?"

"In the car, on the way to Paris?" I tried. No one could have slept through that, but it was a shot at bringing reality back.

"When you were little and strong," Sylvie said. "Lullabies. You liked the French ones best."

It was way too early for someone my age to go to bed on a Friday night but I didn't feel like arguing when she might never sing me a lullaby again. So I gave her a hug and lay in bed for a while, texting Flame about my crazy gran. I remember telling him she was the *best adult in my world. By kilometres.*

Nov 6th

Sylvie's chopped off her hair and it really does make her look mad. She came down to breakfast in her white mules and a long silver dress but we all stared at her raggedy head. It's a bit *quel horreur.*

****

****

Nov 7th

Sylvie's gone. Against her will and mine too.

I hate Dad right now. I wanted to feel a *Railway Children* thrill because he's meant to be my *daddy!* And it's been ages but he only came to take my gran away. He's so reasonable it makes ME mad. And I hate hating him too.

Sylvie didn't know who he was. It was so funny. "It's Pest Control," she said, so I told Zac he'd better hide. Mum kept putting food on the table and talked non-stop, Stu this and Stu that, but after coffee Sylvie said, "Best let the man weed the borders." It was like the best joke ever. She doesn't know her own son is a gardener, but she guessed.

Sad things are the funniest. Or funny things can be really sad.

The usual taxi firm sent a cab.

"It's all right, chérie," she said. "He's such a good driver. He always brings me back on time."

Now she's gone but I didn't cry until I found a little package of peach tissue on my bed. Inside was her hair, for me. It smells of her.

I bet I never see her again.

****
****

Dad managed to keep Sylvie with him and Mireille. We didn't know how, without electronic tagging (Mum's idea). And I dreamed about her getting in that canoe in her long red dress and leopard-print pumps and paddling downriver to South America. My geography's never been the best. But I kept the hair wrapped in tissue paper in my knicker drawer. We're not a *treasures box* kind of family.

I was seeing the counsellor at school once a week but I hate labels so I said as little as possible. "I'm fine," I said. "I have a friend with Alopecia."

"It's no big deal," I said once, ten minutes after I'd been crying in the toilet over a sweaty post-Netball scalp and drippy wig. "It's only hair."

"I'm adjusting," I said. Silence. Change of gear: "It's not like it's terminal!"

I guess the counsellor knew more about drugs and alcohol, anorexia and self-harming. Some of her visitors must have been looking for attention but most people with Alopecia want anything but that, out there in the world. So for her I must have been a challenge like Sylvie, and I think that's what I wanted to be. But I also wanted to be signed off.

The adjusting part wasn't a total lie. I wasn't bullied exactly, like Daisy used to be. People said stupid things that hurt, and some of them still stick. I'm betting there were jokes I never overheard, and nicknames I could guess without much brain strain. But I was lucky.

I wasn't ready to laugh off Alopecia like Daisy but I could get into role. That meant acting tough like my mother but cooler. When I looked in the mirror, I tried to ignore Nancy and zoom in what was left of me: same nose, I-can-pout mouth and good skin. But no eyelashes for mascara to curl and lengthen, and instead of eyebrows I had a couple of beginner's stitches in thin, fair cotton. I did ask Mum to try with kohl one weekend. Her art work was so thick I cried, "I look like a witch! Why don't you brown a few teeth while you're about it?"

I asked Daisy about tattooed eyebrows but she grimaced. I was sleeping over at hers and we were still in dressing gowns

114

eating breakfast, just the two of us, while Molly and Matthew were at church.

"You just don't care, do you?" I asked.

"It's policy," she said. "I suppose I don't believe in caring, not about that."

I told her there's a world out there that judges people by how they look. As if she didn't know.

"It's like everything else," she said. "There's got to be a better way."

I didn't ask much about the better world she wanted. I guess I didn't want to hear all her ideas about the planet, education, celebrity culture and the media in case she asked for mine. I didn't want any, and that was policy too.

"Do you and Flame agree about everything?" I asked, over the sugary cereal they'd bought specially for me.

"No!" She grinned. "He likes Nirvana and Arctic Monkeys!"

I remembered her taste in music: big achey voices, women who sound as if they've been trashed and wounded all through their lives and *ain't taking it no more!*

"You should live with my *lezzy* mother!" I told her.

She looked at me, smile gone. "Don't call her that," she said, quietly.

"My loud, fat, lezzy mother," I said, just to provoke her. "Tell me which bit's not true."

"Don't," Daisy told me. "She doesn't make jokes at your expense."

I was still smiling but it was a bit like catching skin on the cheese grater. So I was relieved when she picked up the local

115

paper, until she saw a headline and smacked it with her knuckles. I wondered whether really she'd like to do that to me.

It was the start of her next campaign.

Nov 27th

OMG Daisy's on a mission. There's a plan to build a car park by the canal in her town, to take overspill from a new supermarket. She reckons it's a wildflower meadow. Except that it's winter so all it's doing is looking messy. She says it's beautiful every spring and summer and the bees and butterflies love it. So now it's *Save The Meadow* as well as *Save the Whale/Arctic/Planet.*

How does she sleep?

How does she ever get an essay done?

No wonder she hasn't got time to flirt with Flame or any other boy.

She's roped him in, and me, and Nina. I'm on promotional materials but she has to proof everything I do. She's such a perfect speller.

I don't get it. What about the shoppers who have to spend half an hour driving round looking for a place to park? No one planted those flowers unless you count the birds. Or God. I think Daisy's a nature worshipper.

"I prefer shoes," I said, but she thinks I'm joking.

Dec 4th

Does Daisy even know it's nearly Christmas? She won't let go of *Flower Power.* That's Flame's name for our little movement. How can I opt out when he's involved? I'd so LOVE to be involved with HIM. I set up a Facebook page and a Twitter account. We've got a Green Euro MP following us, a Native American woman called Prairie Wolf, a folk singer called Angel Morning and just about every group with *Frack* in its name. Daisy's got the Archbishop of Canterbury on her hit list now.

Steve Waterhouse says it's a dead duck, done deal, business matter. Try telling Daisy that. She's calling it *ecocide:* a crime against Earth. Seriously. She reckons if we let the small cases go, the ones on our doorsteps, we've no hope of winning the big ones like the Arctic and the Tar Sands. It's still a scrappy bit of land to me.

She's been in the paper but I refused to pose beside her. Nothing personal. I told the reporter she's the flower round here. I'm just the weed. And I didn't want to be named either, thanks.

I'm busy and it's all right. It gets me out of the house when Val's around. I can't stand the way she disrespects her hair, like she's too busy to brush it, get it shaped or use good conditioner to stop the frizz! It's virtually abuse.

I can't stand the flirty way she talks when she thinks I can't hear. And if Dario takes one step into my room, ecocide won't be the only crime round here.

Polly tweeted today, wishing us good luck. Daisy looked like a cat with a whole bucket of cream.

****
****

Dec 7th

Dee says we're not BFF anymore. I could have said we stopped being BFF the first time she whinged about having a bad hair day.

Mum said she's jealous of Daisy. As if we're still seven.

I wish I *was* seven. Dad would still be here, Mum would be normal (ish) and I'd have the prettiest blonde hair in the class. And I wouldn't know about climate change, ecocide or the arms trade either.

I won't forgive Dee this time. People who always reckon other people are out of order are usually WAY out of order themselves.

****
****

For the first time, I didn't write what I really felt. The diary had no key and Mum did clean my room now and then. I couldn't risk her reading the whole truth about the fall-out with Dee.

Things had been different since I'd been different. I think my Alopecia brought Dee and Yasmin closer just like it united Daisy and me. And it was tough seeing them hanging around school like Siamese twins. In primary school Dee made me laugh, usually by making fun of someone. Teenage Dee still liked to mock people but I had the feeling I was shut out of it – or in the middle, being mocked. Like Maddie Templeton-Adams and her *moustache*; Judith Hebbon and her flab; 'Bert' who was really a girl.

It happened at lunch time. In the dining room Dee offered Judith the lasagne she wouldn't touch, on top of her own. Easy but cruel. Dee pushed out her cheeks in a Judith impression as Judith scoffed the lot.

Outside it was freezing. We both shivered as we sat down on a bench and Dee produced her so-called lunch. I guess a diet of slimming milkshakes can't bring out the best in anyone, whichever celeb swears by them. Dee only had enough flesh to cover her bones without splitting when she bent over. So when she peeled open the pink can as sneakily as a lighting a cigarette, I said she might want to join me for counselling.

"What!" Her eyes narrowed at my wig.

"Eating issues," I suggested, aiming to be gentle and wise. Daisyish. "You're not exactly overweight."

"I'm not planning to be!" She drank some of the shake which smelt sticky-sweet to me. "You want to be careful. Your mum wasn't that fat when we were in primary school and look at her now."

At this point I must have been the one with narrowed eyes. It's a basic rule. Any girl can call her own mother fat or stupid, but the same comments are way out of order when they come from someone else.

"Hey!" I objected. I was getting a flashback to a joke of mine, that if Mum's boobs slung any lower they'd get fried in batter. And the wrong kind of face Dee made then.

"That's probably why she switched sides," said Dee, smiling. "No man would look at her."

That was it. I knocked the can of milkshake out of her hands. Bright pink liquid splashed all over her coat, tights and one shoe. It even caught her dyed auburn fringe.

I wasn't so Daisyish now.

Dee squealed and jumped up from the bench. For a moment I thought she might cry. I remembered us being partners in PE and having a joint birthday party at the ice rink. She used to be so good at plaiting my hair, and telling me how lovely it was. The word she'd just used wasn't in her vocabulary then. Like the word she used next.

"It's not my fault I've got great hair! And it's not my fault your mother's a dyke."

I felt my eyes burn wide. "Don't say one more word about my mother."

Her lips parted but my forefinger was faster, ready to jab. Across the playground Yasmin waved. I knew if I stayed I'd let out words of my own and they'd lead me out of control. I set off across the field even though it was muddy and I was wearing my coolest school shoes.

120

"I wouldn't live with a lesbian! If I was you I'd pack my bags," I heard. "I'd pack my wig."

She couldn't make me turn, or stop, or yell. I felt rain start to target me and my head. Holding my bag above my wig, I turned back and hurried inside. I had no plan or route when I found myself on the corridor, the one that led to the counselling room. I told myself I wouldn't forgive Dee, ever. I knew Yasmin would be told I was the psycho, and see the pink evidence everywhere. So I figured I'd lost two friends for the price of one.

The door has the counsellor's name and qualifications on the metal plate. There are a couple of armchairs outside but I never sat myself on display in what Dee called the Loser Zone, so I always made sure I turned up late for each appointment and walked straight in.

Now I saw Maddie Templeton-Adams spread across one of the leather chairs, reading a Science textbook. She looked up at me. She's got one of those down mouths. Once I said anyone would, with a moustache like that.

"Twelve minutes over. Do you think I should knock?" she asked.

"Someone having a breakdown in there?"

It wasn't really a joke but Maddie looked sad. "Hope not," she said, and grimaced. "How's it going, Rowan?"

I was shocked to be asked, but I realised my own mouth must have taken a dive. I'd never really looked before, but I thought the hair Maddie wore pulled back from her wide, square-jawed face was thick and lush.

"Not having a breakdown anyway!" I said. "You?"

121

"I can't guarantee that myself," she said, seriously. Then she looked hard at me. "Are you all right? You don't look all right."

"Not very," I said. "Just fell out with someone who used to be my best friend. Think it's terminal."

"Maybe she isn't a good enough friend," Maddie suggested.

"Maybe not," I said. "You should be a counsellor yourself."

A group of stunted Y8 boys walked past, glancing at Maddie and me, laughing, muttering. I heard the word 'saddos'. Maddie's face had blotched all over as if she'd been the one running in from the rain.

"I wouldn't be anyone's BFF of choice," she murmured, as the boys turned the corner, still laughing. "But if you ever wanted to… you know, chat, I'm good at listening. I do it to myself."

"Thanks," I said, wishing the door would open.

All of a sudden I was sure Daisy would invite poor Maddie round after school. But I wasn't Daisy and I felt way out on some kind of limb already. I pulled a smile and was wondering how to make an exit when the door did open. A skinny, scruffy Sixth Former shuffled out looking terrible, dark. I remembered Dee calling him a druggie for months and then telling people Ed Carver cut his wrists.

Maddie went in with a smile for him and a "See ya!" for me.

I nearly walked away fast. But it was obvious Ed had been crying, maybe hadn't stopped yet. He wiped his eye with the back of his hand. It made me want to join in. But what would

Daisy have said? I didn't even have a clean tissue to offer him so I just tried to look friendly even though he was scarily tall and his eyes were nearly black, and hot. My Alopecia radar picked up on eyelashes that were long, thick and wet.

Then his watch fell off and managed to land somewhere neither of us could see it.

I heard voices I knew, seconds before I saw Dee and Yasmin approaching. I couldn't believe it. In a huge building overrun by people, it had to be them, catching me out! I looked away, but not before I'd seen the way they blanked me.

"Birds of a feather," said Dee, and smiled, touching her head. "Or none."

I knew she'd think she'd been clever even though she looked like a flamingo herself. She hadn't made a very good job of wiping her sweatshirt.

"Excuse my ex-friends," I said, remembering the boy's real name: Ed Carter. Carver was just Dee's joke.

His eyes were following the pair of them now, as if he'd forgotten the missing watch. Then he looked back at me. "Don't let them make you small," he said.

He had about eight inches on me but I didn't think he was being funny. Then we walked away, in opposite directions.

My joke. I remembered now. I could hear myself cracking it: 'Ed Carver'. So quick, so sharp. Only it wasn't funny. I wondered whether his sleeves caught on thin red cuts and that made me wince too. It also reminded me of the new tampon I'd need before afternoon lessons began.

In the toilets I found Ed Carter's watch in my bag. If I'd fancied him, it would have been a rom-com kind of opportunity. As it was, I thought my best chance was Mrs O in the office. I explained and she put it in an envelope.

"Poor lad," she said, but I knew there was no point in asking why. "I saw your name in the paper, Rowan." I'm sure I didn't look pleased, even though she seemed to be fully signed up to *Flower Power*. "Good for you and your friend Daisy," she said. "More people should get off their backsides and leave their cars at home. Then we wouldn't need extra car parks. It'd cut the traffic queues and the pollution."

"Mm," I said. I wasn't much of a walker.

"And what's wrong with buses anyway? I don't know what's worse – the laziness or the snobbery!"

She said I'd set her off on her *high horse* so I joked that a bike might be less trouble than one of those and she laughed quite loudly.

"You're doing really well now, Rowan," she said, with one of her soft smiles. "You should be proud of yourself."

I probably looked embarrassed. I nearly said she might not think so if school had CCTV. I knew she didn't mean eco campaigning. She meant Alopecia – only sometimes you'd think the word was on the banned list.

I smiled and said, "Thanks, Mrs O."

"I'll make sure Ed Carter knows who to thank!" she called as I hurried off.

It's not easy when your ex-BFF is behind you in a lesson and you imagine the lasers aimed between your shoulders. For the rest of the day I just kept my eyes on walls, clocks, even teachers.

Nina sent me a surprise text as I walked home, about a song she was learning, asking whether I knew it, and I told her it was a pig of a day. So she rang, asking if she could help – a bit like a receptionist on a desk. I told her everything and even though she didn't have a lot to say, I heard sympathy with a bit of outrage. But I told her I could tough this out like everything else.

Dee didn't send a *sorry* and even if she had, I wasn't in the mood to forget anything. When I heard by text from Daisy, who'd been out, I told her I was off to bed and turned off my phone, wishing Flame was the one who cared.

10

Dec 13th

I've been busy. *Flower Power* just got wild. Overgrown.
Daisy's been working on it for a bit without telling me, didn't
think I was that committed. Don't know where she got that
idea. Anyway it all came together in a crazy flash mob dancing
to an old hippy song about watching flowers in the rain.
Dressed as flowers obviously. And bees. Seriously. Frances
came dressed as a daffodil in a bonnet, whirling and wiggling
her fingers. Lots of mums with kids. I was just audience but I
said I'd see to the filming and music.

Even in furry black and yellow stripes Daisy kicked ass.
That nutter can move. And she's happy with the impact,
coverage and all that. She reckons we've won. Yeah right. It's
that easy in Daisy's world. A bit of commitment and big
business just lies down and rolls over.

****
****

Dec 15th

Might as well cancel Christmas. I can't see the point. Dad will be having a *joyeux Noël* with Mireille, Sylvie and *possiblement* the *bébé* too. I'd rather change nappies than be here in my own home with Val and the brat invading. I'd put up Zac's musty Cub tent in the garden but they're forecasting snow. And that's NOT romantic.

I wish Flame would hurry up and realise he's madly in love with me. A green reggae Christmas in London would be cool. Any Christmas would be cool with Flame.

****
****

Dec 17th

OMG I'm so sick.

Flame is with Nina, not me. Not Daisy, either, but she's making out it's just a musical collaboration on some Ecocide song he's written and wants Nina to sing.

Why didn't Mum hand down her voice instead of her no-way mouth and a fierce forefinger?

Bet deep down Daisy wishes she was the one collaborating over Flame's keyboards.

Flame and Nina. I can't get it out of my head. Bet they're an item not a double act. Or soon will be.

I'd be prettier than Nina if I had hair, and I'm a lot sharper. She'd better watch out.

****
****

Dec 18th

Ooooooh! I have a brand new sister (half) like I've always wanted. Matilde Amelie. She looks gorgeous in that squishy red way. She'll probably be a nicer daughter than me. I hope she keeps all that soft fair hair.

****
****

Dec 19th

When exactly was my mother planning to tell me? I had to overhear Val, yattering downstairs about estate agents and the value of our house. And how lovely it will be when they're together.

NOT FOR ME IT WON'T.

I yelled at Mum but I can't get through. She says it makes no sense, money-wise. We're moving in next-door as soon as we can find a buyer. OR SO SHE THINKS. I'm not going anywhere. I'll get a pet rat to keep under my bed and let it out of the cage when people come to view. I'll throw ketchup at the lounge walls if I have to. It's my home and I won't give it up.

This has been the worst year of my life. And it's not over yet.

****
****

So I followed my ex-BBF's advice and packed my suitcase. I went to stay with Daisy the day term finished. I heard Val tell Mum it would give me space to cool off and get used to their plans.

"I won't get USED to anything," I told Val on the landing as I passed with a clutch of bags, "but I'll get AWAY from here. I might not come back."

"Oh, Rowan," she said, "I know change is difficult, but your mum and I love each other. I just want to make her happy."

Downstairs Mum wasn't happy. It showed through her loud, jokey front as she offered everyone tea and cake. But that was fine by me because I didn't want her to be happy. I expected Zac to give me the evil eye as if I was some kind of traitor. But in fact he was getting on much better with Dario and they were in the middle of some game, so he could hardly be bothered to stop to say goodbye.

I'd asked Daisy if her nice step-dad Matthew could pick me up, because I didn't want to be with Mum in the car. The stay was meant to be a week at the most but I left my room half-stripped.

At the door Matthew was too nice. He invited Mum to come and visit and when I said she'd be too busy she said she would, thanks. And told me to be good.

"Bye," I said, keeping my distance. But Daisy was there behind me, willing me to give Mum a hug. So I let it happen when I might have ducked it. The large body pressed against me was very warm and smelt of chips as usual.

Daisy's spare room is small but thanks to Molly the walls are painted with poppies and butterflies. I said it was like the meadow we were trying to save.

"I know you'll want space sometimes," said Daisy, "but don't feel alone."

"I won't," I said.

"And if you change your mind and want to go home, just say."

"I won't."

That evening we put up the decorations and lit tea lights, like a family. It felt peaceful and Christmassy, and I told myself as I fell asleep in the meadow room that I was glad to be there. My wig settled right in, making itself at home by the side of my bed on Daisy's disused stand. I realised it was looking a bit faded and ragged already. Life was taking a toll on Nancy. And I wasn't expecting a state-of-the-art replacement from Santa.

Over those few days I did a few things I'd never done before. First we went carol singing to raise money for the local hospice. Daisy wore a mad pineapple-shaped woolly hat to keep her head warm but there was no way I was going to squash my wig. My singing was shivery as well as flat – unlike Nina's. She could audition for an angel choir. But it was hard to hate her too much because she was so gentle with me, like a nurse with a sick child.

It started raining towards the end but I tried not to be too sulky. Afterwards we all had hot cinnamon punch and mince pies at a mansion with acres of gardens and about five bathrooms, owned by a woman with a duchess voice. People put their umbrellas in some sort of Chinese china stand, so big I could have shoved Nina right inside.

"Why doesn't the duchess write a cheque for a couple of thousand pounds and save all this trouble?" I asked Daisy, having a snoop from the hallway.

"You sound like Flame," said Daisy.

"Is he a revolutionary?" I asked. I had a vague idea that Che Guevara had been sexy.

"Only a peaceful one," said Daisy.

We both looked at Nina then. "I don't like to talk politics," she said. "It's too sad and too scary."

You sing politics, I thought. If I was with Flame I wouldn't need to talk at all, just look at him and enjoy him looking back… but not at my wig. I tried not to imagine him running his long brown fingers through Nina's hair. It might not be silk-gloss but it'd feel a lot softer than my clumpy acrylic.

The Waterhouse crew walked Nina home afterwards, to her crummy flat in a street where the grass was for dog poo and fag ends. Flame called just as we were saying goodbye and Nina's whole face shone in the darkness. Even though she passed her phone over to Daisy first and then to me, so we could all say *hi*, I felt suddenly sad. I didn't belong and I wasn't anyone's first choice anywhere.

Back at Daisy's, Molly said it would be OK to Skype Dad and talk to my sister but no one picked up. When she said of course I could call Mum any time, I said she'd be out singing. I'd already ignored three texts and answered the fourth with a *Fine*.

Molly and Matthew hurried out to a party and Daisy said if I wanted to choose, we could watch a DVD. She left me searching for a title I'd heard of and came back downstairs in red tartan pyjamas. I couldn't help grinning at the sight of her because she still wore her dangly frog earrings, and her head looked paler and smaller than usual.

"Take your wig off if you like," she said. "No one to see."

It didn't sound pre-meditated. She was almost casual. I felt my face redden. "I don't."

The house was cosy; the solar panels were doing a good job. But now I wrapped my cardigan round me as if I was cold. I felt tight and shaken.

Daisy asked if I wanted to make a smoothie.

"Not if it's broccoli and banana," I said, and she laughed. When she reached for the peanut butter she gave me a cheeky grin so I told her to behave. Then she made me shut my eyes so I could identify the ingredients when I drank. I told her no chillies and cooperated, sniffing loudly for clues.

"You know that question," I began, not sure whether I wanted to follow through, "about what you'd save if the house was on fire?"

"Yeah?" she asked, over the noise. Was I asking or admitting? She knew before I did. "Your wig?"

I nodded.

"Not a photo of someone you've lost?" she asked, and I remembered that she'd lost her granddad too and might have loved him more than I loved either of mine.

"No," I said. Then I knew it wasn't true. "I'd save a photo of me, with my own hair."

Someone I've lost, I thought, and Daisy may have thought it too because she's usually a step ahead. I started telling her about my favourite picture of me, at my Brummie uncle's wedding, all dressed up just before Alopecia got a hold.

"What about you?" I asked eventually, not sure I wanted to hear the answer.

"Oh," she said, pouring a greeny-orange liquid into glasses. "I suppose if I had to choose one thing it would be a scrapbook of cuttings from the paper about saving Katya."

Another Polish waif? It took a moment but then I remembered the whale.

"As a reminder – of what human beings can do when they work together. Katya. It's our code for never give up."

Our. That meant Flame. I supposed they were like brother and sister but I was jealous all the same.

Watching her take the blender to the sink, I thought of another answer to my own question: Sylvie's hair, for me. I started to tell Daisy, but then I stopped. "I haven't even brought it with me!"

It was still in my knicker drawer, waiting for me to end my protest and go home.

"It's the love behind the gift that matters," Daisy said, "not the gift."

It wasn't the line I'd taken when my birthday and Christmas presents were cheaper or less cool than the ones I'd asked for. But now I was feeling a bit churned up, like the smoothie. Daisy hugged me.

"Tell me there's no peanut butter in this," I said, and she only grinned. She felt much hotter than me in spite of her bare head.

I'd left a scattering of DVDs on the carpet. I could tell she wanted to watch a movie about Death Row and a nun but I chose one her dad had given her – "to give me a break from caring!" And dumb was good, because we didn't need to pay attention so we kept talking.

Then just before ten, she took a text which she read aloud: "Flame: *Armed Conflict: made in Britain. On in five, C4.*"

At that point the on-screen hero was surrounded by laser-toting robots but Steve Waterhouse was right. I really *didn't* care. Daisy cared all right – about arms manufacturers on industrial estates near YOU.

"We can't stop people making weapons," I said.

"Just because it's big business, that doesn't make it right. Children die." And she started listing countries that bought

British arms so they could kill their own people. I wondered why she needed to watch the programme if she already knew so much about it.

I decided I didn't need to know, and went to bed.

Next morning I didn't expect to escape a blow-by-blow account of the documentary, but I got a lot more. She was up already, tracking down the arms manufacturers on *her* doorstep. Molly Waterhouse worked at an art shop and got to bring home card that was too bent to sell, leaky paints and all kinds of slightly shop-soiled bits and pieces, which it turned out Daisy kept under my bed. So she'd been waiting for me to wake up so she could pull it all out and start making a placard.

She was so obsessive it was almost funny. While I ate breakfast in front of the TV, she was measuring, cutting, sticking and producing fancy lettering with thick waterproof pens.

ARMS MANUFACTURER, it said.

"I wanted to put DICTATORS WELCOME underneath," she said, "or CHILD KILLERS. Flame said best not."

"Is he coming?" I asked, probably looking a bit like a child who's been told Santa's been sighted at the end of the street.

"He'll join me later," she said, and looked up from her taping. "Or us?"

"Is it... you know, legal?" I asked.

"It shouldn't be!"

"Not them," I said. "Us!"

"Depends," she said. "Probably. Unless they give us no choice."

Molly had gone to work but I guessed she must know. Daisy was so fired up she hadn't slept. I wasn't sure anyone could have stopped her. But she sat down with me, turned off the TV and told me what we were going to do: stand outside this arms manufacturing company that didn't admit to being one, take a photo and get it all round the web. In fact, when Flame arrived it could become a film on YouTube.

"What will they do – these people in the factory place?" I asked.

"They won't open fire!" She grinned. "They might get heavy but we won't move."

"You mean ever?" I looked out of the window onto a grey sky that could be getting ready to rain on us, or even cover us in snow. I saw and heard a gust of wind that was bound to be cold.

"Nothing will change unless we try to change it," she said. She reckoned that arms companies sponsored Science Fairs for kids and museums, that royals were roped in to do the deals with countries like Saudi Arabia, and that if Britain was prepared to sell to just about anyone we couldn't object if British weapons killed our soldiers.

I'd never thought about it but I couldn't see a reason to argue, except fear. And Daisy apparently didn't have any.

That's how we ended up getting the bus with our placard. Daisy carried that, and a flask of tea and sandwiches in her backpack along with what she called kit. At the other end we had to walk what she described as not far and I was soon calling miles. The industrial estate looked boring and ugly the way they do, and seemed quiet. Plenty of cars were parked, but we couldn't actually see anyone who belonged there. I thought there might be barbed wire or look-out towers like POW camps in movies with Nazis, but the place might have been making oven gloves or scented candles for all you could tell.

Daisy had done her research. I only tagged along, just about keeping up, until we reached a sign. The name gave nothing away and it wasn't as if the symbol was a machine gun or a bomb exploding. But Daisy soon fixed that, as soon as she'd handed me the placard. In her kit bag was a tube of red paint that you squeeze on like icing. She began to apply artwork to look like blood dripping from the letters of the company name. It was cool but really horrible, and so quick I wondered whether she'd practised all night. My mouth opened wide. I looked nervously around us. Nothing, not yet.

"Quick," she said, putting the paint away and taking the placard again. "Photo."

It was my turn to act fast, on video setting. Just as well, really, because at that moment we heard a shout.

"Oy! Girlies!"

It was meant to be loud and growly. I shoved the phone in my pocket. Both the men were burly and bearded, but not as fit as they should be. We had a hundred metres on our side so I was pretty sure we could outrun them. But glancing at Daisy I could see she wasn't going anywhere. In fact she sat right down with the placard held in both hands against her chest.

It's not as if we were in a park. There was no seat, or even any grass, because the only surface was the concrete driveway where vehicles came and went. I was wearing my best cream coat but I had no choice. I felt safer next to Daisy, the two of us squished into one like the weeds spouting up against the fence behind us.

"What the _____ do you think you're doing?" cried one, the fatter and shorter of the two. I could smell his aftershave.

"Haven't you got pressies to wrap?" asked his mate. "Time to go home now. Up you get. NOW."

"We're staying put for now," said Daisy calmly, with a bright smile. She produced the flask. "I'd offer you a cuppa but this has to last us all day."

All day! I hoped she was bluffing. The ground was cold. The wind was what Mum called 'more biter than bitter'. I noticed one of them looking at Daisy's hat as if he'd worked out that there was no hair underneath it. Then he glanced at my wiggy head. I thought he was processing data but I wasn't sure whether it meant they'd go soft on us or pull Nancy off and jeer in my face.

"Enjoy your picnic," he said. "Then we'll have to escort you off-site, and clean up." He looked up at the sign. "That's criminal damage."

"It's an illustration," said Daisy, "Making it clearer to the community what the company's business involves." She poured tea slowly into the little cup and passed it to me. "*Damaging* people, spilling blood." It was tea she'd spilt on me. "Murder and ecocide: they're the crimes."

"We'll see what the police have to say about that," said the shorter one. "How old are you girls?"

"The press always want to know that too," said Daisy. "Tea all right?" she asked me and I said, "Yeah, it's good thanks."

The taller man backed off and Mr Nasty seemed puzzled but followed. They made sure we could still see them, chatting quietly, considering the problem. Daisy didn't look, though. She was digging out the sandwiches.

"Can't we go?" I asked. "We've made our point." I was watching the men, trying to read them while they tried to read us.

"Don't let them think we're intimidated," she murmured. "Flame will be here soon."

She offered me her scarf but it wouldn't have worked with the coat. Or anything else in my wardrobe.

"Why are we doing this?" I asked. "We can't stop war."

"That's what people told Wilberforce about slavery. I know we can't close the place down, not today or even tomorrow, but the people in this town have the right to know what's manufactured here."

"They won't care," I said. I was pretty sure there were more people like me than Daisy.

"We're giving them the chance to care. We're saying things will only change if you want them to. It's one action but that's how anything begins."

I thought people were more likely to try to stop a wind farm than arms dealers but I didn't tell her that. She was full of faith in humanity and I didn't have much myself.

"I dragged you along," she said. "Sorry. But it'll be all over the Internet. I'm guessing it's happening everywhere, at places like this right across the UK."

So I was part of a movement, a news item! Dee and Yasmin would fall off their sofas. But I would have liked one of those to sit on myself. The food helped but the tea was soon gone and I didn't like to ask what happened if either of us needed the loo.

Then Daisy's phone rang and her face brightened as she cried, "Flame!" But the smile faded as she listened. He wasn't coming because he was at his nearest arms manufacturer with his mum and he had to keep her company because they couldn't find anyone else who could go. And Daisy had me.

"Some movement," I muttered.

Daisy tried to sound fine about it but I could see she wasn't, and when she ended the call and told me it made sense, I knew sense had nothing to do with feelings.

"OK," she said suddenly, "can you film me explaining? We'll put it on YouTube ourselves."

I brushed the crumbs off my coat as I stood, hoping this meant we were filming and then calling it a day. The phone was still on, and I wasn't sure whether in the darkness of my pocket it had picked up any sound. Daisy was standing too, placard positioned so that I could frame it with the company sign. She began, but fluffed something and asked to start again.

As I filmed her, speech-making, I saw in her eyes how deep this went for her, and the passion was a kind of shock. But not as much of a shock as the two security guards running heavily towards us, shouting. There were two men in business suits behind them, leaving them to sprint as best they could but scuttling after them. Daisy's look meant me to carry on, but wouldn't they just grab my phone and smash it? I waited until I could smell the aftershave again. Then I shoved the phone between my tight little jumper and bra.

The tall man grabbed me by the wrist. The short one shoved Daisy in the chest, pushing her against the fence. She held on to the placard and part of me wanted her to smack it down on heads, because the guy who'd got my arm in his grip was giving me a kind of airport search with his other palm, only much rougher. I screamed, trying to push him away with my free hand.

"Let go of her!" Daisy yelled. "You're hurting her, you bullies. You have no right to touch us!"

I was trying to break free, kicking. I was about to knee him where it would hurt most when we heard the car. And another! No sirens, but it was the police. Of course the company had called them but those two employees of theirs were quick to let us go and step back, looking professional and in charge.

"Thank you for coming, officers," said Daisy. "You're witnesses to assault."

"Rowan?" I heard.

That came from another cop, stepping out of the second car. It was Yasmin's dad. Last time I'd seen him he was dressed in a tiger onesie she'd given him for his birthday, eating his breakfast in their kitchen. I'd forgotten his job, if I ever knew what it was. He looked at me and my wig and I wondered how much he knew.

We just waited, the two of us, while the men talked. One cop car drove off to find some proper criminals. Daisy did some dance moves to keep warm but I wasn't *that* cold. I did suggest, "We could do a runner!" but Daisy only smiled. I told her more about Dee and Yasmin, including things I'd never told anyone, the most hurtful things – and how happy I was in Paris with Sylvie.

Because I wasn't sixteen yet, they had to call an adult and that meant Mum. Yasmin's dad said we could sit in the police car but I couldn't abandon Daisy and she still wasn't moving. I couldn't see why. It was over.

I cringed when Mum arrived in the van, still in her fat-splashed overalls and caterer's hat. She wanted to know what Molly was doing letting us 'get up to a stunt like this'. Daisy was super-calm and polite with her, but she explained how important it was that people stood up for their beliefs.

Mum looked at me, as if to say, what beliefs would those be?

"I agree with Daisy," I said.

"There's taking action," she said, "and there's going way too far."

"These weapons go a long way," I said, fired up myself now, "and blow people up in the streets."

"You can look closer for people going way too far," said Daisy, and told her how we'd been pushed around and grabbed.

That was when the words *red rag* and *bull* sprang to mind. A couple of security guards soon found a Jools Figg forefinger aimed at their faces, probably smelling of onion and vinegar. She wanted an apology, she demanded to see their boss and she'd certainly be pressing charges for assault. She told them a company like this might have good lawyers but she could assure them they wouldn't be good enough.

"SHAME!" she cried, moving in on their personal space, "ON – YOU!"

The bosses tried to put her down and/or shut her up with long words and smooth private school voices but they were wasting their breath.

"That's enough from you," she said, finger out again. "More than enough."

Cue for police intervention. But by this point I really, really needed a pee. I told Daisy. I was invited to use the washroom over the fence in the arms place but I didn't need Daisy's eyes on me to supply my answer to that.

"I'd rather wet myself, thanks."

Daisy said she was desperate too. It turned out that the nearest building on the industrial estate was rented by the local hospice as a pre-loved furniture store, and the female officer escorted Daisy and me to ask if we could use the Ladies. As we walked the woman asked about the *Flower Power* campaign and Daisy was happy to tell her.

We left the policewoman in the reception area, chatting. It turned out that her aunt had been in the hospice and we left her buying a ticket for a Christmas concert.

Once the door was shut behind us, Daisy pointed to my chest. Her eyes widened. Maybe it crossed both our minds that if this was a movie, we wouldn't be allowed to leave that site with the phone still safely out of reach down my bra. And full of video evidence.

Daisy produced a jiffy bag from her kit. It was addressed to Flame and stamped. I was so panicked and in such urgent need now that I just dropped my phone inside and went first into the cubicle. When I came out again I couldn't ask her what I was supposed to do without my phone over Christmas, in case we were overheard. I just had to trust Daisy. It was like a dream except that even my bad ones were normally more real than this.

We were escorted back to our local arms factory, where everything seemed to have quietened down, even Mum. In fact, apart from Daisy's art work there was no sign of any unusual activity at all. The bosses and heavies had disappeared and the police car was parked further back on the road. We didn't ask what had been settled, if anything. Mum was chatting with Yasmin's dad and I had a feeling it might be about the fall-out. Maybe Mum was thinking that I wouldn't be in this mess with Dee or Yasmin. And remembering my phone, I began to think Daisy was deranged after all.

Mum said she hoped we'd agree with her that we'd done enough. I had, personally. I'd exceeded anything I'd ever imagined, but I wasn't sure about Daisy.

"I'd drive you back home," continued Mum. "But there's only room for one in the van."

"I can get the bus," said Daisy, "thanks, Julie."

"Me too," I said. "I'm going back to Daisy's."

"Do you want to hand over your phone, love?" asked the female cop, hand out. "We don't want any more trouble now."

"We'd be interested to see any footage," said Yasmin's dad.

"They can't make you, Rowan!" cried Daisy. She's quite an actress.

But so am I when I have to be. I placed my hand over my coat pocket and froze. I gave Daisy a look I knew they'd see. As if I was trying to be furtive, I switched to the other pocket.

I swore. "I couldn't give it you if I wanted to!" I cried, sounding a bit hysterical. "I don't believe it! I put it in my coat pocket, after those thugs tried to grope me!" Remembering that, it was easy enough to cry. I reached, fumbled, gave myself a body search and swore again. "I've gone and lost it now! It'd better not have fallen down the loo."

The WPC who wanted to be called Jan started heading back to retrace our steps so I guessed she was fooled.

"Rowan, you're kidding," moaned Daisy. I don't know which of us was more convincing.

"Don't have a go at me," I said. "It's *my* phone!" I was sniffing and wiping my nose with my hand so Mum gave me a hankie. "I didn't want to come in the first place," I told her.

Daisy was looking disgusted with me. "It was all for nothing, then," she said quietly.

Her backpack was behind her, like they tend to be, but for a moment I thought Yasmin's dad might be less of a pushover and want to search it. But he didn't. I could only guess at the scenes in his house if Yasmin lost her phone, which I'd been known to say I'd die for.

Mum was probably ashamed. She'd gone quiet but she hadn't left. WPC Jan called Yasmin's dad to report that there was no sign of the phone in the hospice furniture store.

"Mum, I need a new phone," I groaned, shivering and making my teeth rattle.

"We'll find it if it's here," said Yasmin's dad, "and let you know. I'll drop you girls at the bus stop. Unless…?"

"My things are at hers," I said. "Come round tonight, Mum, yeah?"

"All right, love," she said.

I realised my acting had been too good. Now Mum thought I'd had enough of Daisy and would be packing again. I didn't say a word on the short drive to the bus stop in the police car. Daisy only mumbled with a wounded edge that Mum must be glad I'd decided to go home for Christmas. Then Yasmin's dad left us with advice to forget today, make up all round and enjoy a good *Chrimbo*.

There was a post box just a few feet away from the bus stop. As soon as he'd driven on, Daisy ran to it and dropped the package through the slot. She hurried back again, backpack swinging behind her. I was just wondering whether it was safe to talk, or even smile, when a car pulled up on the other side of the road. The police car, which Yasmin's dad must just have turned round. A few seconds later and he would have caught us congratulating ourselves. Or me passing out with relief.

He crossed towards us. I remembered to glare at Daisy.

"Daisy," he said, "you don't suppose that phone found its way into your bag?"

"I don't see how," said Daisy, swinging it over her shoulders and unzipping. She rummaged, shaking her head. Then she produced the paint and joked, "You got me bang to rights!"

He held out his hands and she looked offended as he pulled the backpack towards him. He searched through it, thoroughly.

"All right," he said. "Just a thought. Don't get yourselves in any more deep water, all right? You don't want to mess with people like that. Off the record."

He crossed back to the car. "Hope Santa brings you a new one, Rowan!" he called.

And off he drove.

Dec 21st

I'm home now. Mum came for supper at Daisy's and afterwards I packed my bag. It was quite emotional hugging Daisy because of the crazy day we had. Which I won't go into in case this diary ever ends up as evidence.

O... M... G!

****

****

Dec 22nd

Daisy messaged me today: *Bodhisattva! X*

Who needs training? I'm a naturally enlightened being. The next text said I'm more of a Shambhala warrior really so I looked it up and apparently they/we(!) are the people with the sacred wisdom to solve the world's problems. In my case, more scared than sacred.

Of course I have to use my old laptop to do all this stuff as I seem to have mislaid my phone!

Apart from me reaching for that phone a hundred times, today's been so normal it's weird. Mum's decided that her customers should all be eating nothing but mince pies by now, so she's started her holiday. We went shopping but split up for a bit and met for coffee after I'd bought her something nice.

Hope she hasn't got me a new phone!

11

Daisy doesn't believe in forgiveness! That's what she told me last Christmas, just as the dust settled on our *action* and we didn't know how long it would be before it swirled around again.

"What?" I asked, on the landline. I knew I must have missed something.

"Because when people love you they don't mean to get things wrong or hurt you so there's nothing to forgive. They're just being human."

Now it makes more sense. But I told myself I hadn't really forgiven Mum, not completely. I was just letting her off for now, giving her a bit of a break because I needed to, after everything that had happened. So underneath I was still holding a grudge. We didn't talk much about my short time at Daisy's. Maybe what I did on that industrial estate was so out of character she couldn't process it. I was having trouble with that myself. I got the feeling she didn't know whether to feel proud or panic-stricken, which was pretty much the same as me.

Zac kept asking questions. "Are you going to prison?" at breakfast didn't help.

"No one's going to touch her!" Mum cried, from the frying pan. "If I had the money, I'd take those thugs to the cleaner's and shut that place down! But if you're going to become some kind of anarchist, young lady, I might have to get you tagged and tap your phone!"

"I haven't GOT a phone!" I moaned, because by this time I was missing it badly and I'd just squirted myself in the eye with grapefruit juice.

As Mum served up Zac's cooked breakfast, I tried to explain the difference between Daisy and an anarchist. "That's like calling an armpit a coconut just because it's hairy!"

I'd stolen that from Daisy. Mum looked at me and grinned. Then she laughed out loud and I thought she was never going to stop. Zac and I rolled eyes at each other. Christmas must have been in the air because he offered me a bit of the sausage I'd been eyeing. Mum wiped her eyes, washed her hands and disappeared suddenly, returning with her own phone. She put it down in front of me: her slightly greasy, practically antique model, clunky and chunky, not a single frill.

"Short-term loan," she said. "We'll think again after Christmas. You can call and text, only when you have to." She was still on Pay-As-You-Go. "In the unlikely event of anyone wanting me you can give me a shout."

I gave it the kind of look I used to give any boiled egg she expected me to eat when I was little because the white made me gag.

"I can't work this," I said.

"You're studying History, aren't you?"

I fetched the anti-bacterial spray. I think I managed a thank you once I'd worked out how to save in some of the contact numbers I knew by heart: Daisy's and Flame's.

"Yasmin would like to hear from you," Mum remarked.

"Is that right?" I remembered Yasmin's number, too, but I hesitated. I told Mum she'd been a bitch like Dee and in any case she hated me now. I asked Mum why it mattered to her anyway and she said she didn't believe in giving up on people.

"Only men," I said.

"But not boys!" cried Zac.

I think Mum meant us to share the wink. It was big enough.

"Some people deserve to be dropped," I said. "Some people ask for it."

Mum reminded us that as it was Christmas Eve, Brummie Gran was coming round for lunch. And that later on we were going to do something special, something we'd both enjoy and Gran too. So that meant Val wasn't involved because Gran acted as if Val didn't exist.

"Trust me," Mum said, "you'll have fun. You can both bring a friend along."

Dec 24th

Went to an amazing Christmas party at the hospice. Mum had it set up with Daisy, and Zac took Dario. It's like they're blood brothers now.

The decorations were incredible, a bit like the West End but indoors. The comedian was quite good and the magician was fatter than Santa but cool. Mum sang with some old guy on piano. I had to run to the loo when she started OMG hip swerves on *Santa Baby* but in the Ladies I could still hear her. Like anyone on the street. When I came out Brummie Gran was swaying and clapping with her eyes all cloudy.

I had this horrible thought. The audience was full of people who could die soon, and people who love them. That must be so weird. Daisy said the hospice would be a happy place to die but there's no such thing, is there?

She got chatting the way she does, with one family. She had to tell them straight away she hasn't got cancer because Debbie has. She's so thin she makes Nina look obese. She can't be much older than forty and she was really nice to us. "You must be proud of your mum," she told me. OMG! Her kids must be SO proud of *her* and she won't be there next Christmas.

John's seventeen but obviously he likes Daisy better than me. He's got thick curly hair Dee would call girly and glasses she'd call sad. And a kind smile. Maybe having a dying mother makes you a better person. It must stop you worrying about the stupid things. His sister (Louisa) is only thirteen. OF COURSE she looked up to Daisy and told her how brave she is. We should get T-shirts: I'M BRAVE for Daisy and I'M NOT for me. I could see Louise might cry any time, even when she was laughing at the jokes. Just as well Mum didn't sing *Silent Night* because Debbie will soon be sleeping in *heavenly peace.* OMG so sad. I don't know how they bear it. But Louisa said it was a great party like she meant it.

Daisy's just been picked up for a midnight service. I told her to say a prayer for Debbie.

0:17 so it's Christmas now.

****
****

Dec 25th

Can't believe it. Mum gave me an amazing new phone. It's way better than the old one. I didn't tell her what happened to mine, not today.

I put a few numbers in and sent *Happy Christmas* to them all. Including Dee. She sent straight back: *U2 Rowan X.* Mum winked when I showed her. It's good when you get back your past after you thought it was trashed but if I have a BFF now it's Daisy, who else? Sometimes everything changes.

Val brought the boys for lunch but it was OK. Val looks quite royal in a dress and heels so Gran decided to talk to her. Mum wore Val's present: a cool black Whitby Jet necklace. She reckons it sets off the gorilla slippers I bought her.

I helped cook. Mum says it's good to know she can retire one day and leave *Reckless* in safe hands. NOOOOOOO! I might be a nurse. Or a midwife. I like babies, esp. my Matilde. She's going to love me. We Skyped and she's smiling. So cute! I can't wait to cuddle her like Sylvie did. I think my granny recognised me and she blew me lots of kisses but she only called me *chérie*.

I hope Flame had a good one. Can't wait to cuddle him too. That would be in my dreams.

****
****

Dec 26th

OMG I did it! Can't believe I did. I blame the mulled wine!

Went to Daisy's for the BIG party in Val's people carrier. Daisy says Boxing Day gets bigger every year. Aunts, uncles, cousins, grandparents… and Molly's best friend Liz (looking like a fortune teller) with her late-life husband. She's a Scottish feminist who jangles with bangles and fell in love when she was really old. It's their little blonde toddler who has Daisy for a godmother. Just like I do – HAHA!

Steve Waterhouse rolled up with slick hair and a girlfriend Daisy says he's been keeping quiet. Melissa may be off-the-peg normal now, but she's got no idea! Crazy Daise will have her waving a banner by New Year.

The lounge was hot and heaving even before Flame and Kyle arrived. I swear he looked straight at me, best smile on the planet. Wish I could have caught it on my phone. Too busy melting.

Nina arrived later with her mum, dad and sister. So in the kitchen and hallway we ended up squeezing round each other.

It was a bit like when lines are closed at weekends on the underground and passengers on the tubes that ARE running get a bit too intimate. Not intimate enough for me as far as Flame's concerned.

It's not like the lounge is the size of a football pitch. I hate sweating and I don't want a drippy wig, thanks. Flame and Daisy made room for dancing (pretty OMG amazing) and it was so loud and buzzing and Christmassy by then, I wanted to let go too. I hadn't planned it. I would have said I'd rather eat things with six legs (all still moving). If I'd thought about it for two seconds it would never have happened. But I took Nancy off. Right in the middle of the room. And the OMG feeling came too late, once it was there in my hand. Instead of on my head.

It needs care like a pet so I wasn't going to shove it in my bag. I just held it a second, as if I didn't know what to do with it. Daisy took it and put it upstairs on that old stand of hers. But only after she'd hugged me.

You know what Flame said in my ear – or shouted really, above Steve Waterhouse's favourite song called (OMG) *Don't you want me, baby?* "Cool, Rowan, seriously cool!"

And I felt it.

But I haven't started some kind of habit. And if anyone posts a photo on FB I might have to kill her!

****
****

Dec 27th

Flame and Nina put their Ecocide song on YouTube. OK, so Nina's voice is haunting. People say it gives them chills but who needs those? There must be some bored people out there with time on their hands because so far it's had 764 views. In ten hours.

Yes, Daisy, I know they're not bored really. They care about the earth and every living thing on it including young people who don't want a life of climate chaos thanks very much. Or they're swooning over Flame like me.

Talked to Matilde on screen. She's not very chatty yet. But Sylvie was asleep. I bet she partied too hard over Christmas. Dad says she's even more confused now there's another girl in the family. It's SO sad.

Gran's at my Brummie uncle's now and we weren't invited. I think he's a homophobe but I never liked him anyway. Val cooked lunch at her house. Show-off. She had to do a low-fat gourmet feast but Mum seemed to love it. I suppose that's because she loves Val. Daisy says (she would!) maybe I'll find out what it is she loves, if I give Val a chance. I said that's what I'm doing. Dario needs a slap though. He grinned and said, "You were *bald* last night," as if I didn't know. So I said, "I'm bald *every* night, Dario, and every day too. That's what makes me so special."

Sharp, right? But Mum outclassed me. "No," she said, finger in action, "it's just one of the things that make you special." For a hard nut she can be soggy with a couple of sherries inside her.

Flame didn't get any post. With Christmas delays it could be weeks. Thank you very much, Daisy. My new phone is amazing though. I can play him (and the ecocide song) on it whatever room I'm in, on a loop. And I do. Oh yes…

****
****

Dec 28th

OMG!!!

I slept in but a phone call woke me. From Flame: the perfect alarm clock. The postie had brought him a package! "It's a bit shaky," he said, "but incredible!"

My undercover footage! Kyle knows someone who can get the sound right up so you hear everything. Two hours later it was on YouTube (yeah, we rule the Internet) and there's a line in the Ecocide song about war and weapons so it's a kind of intro and then it's all there, me and Daisy, and red paint, standing up to the heavy mob. Dead incriminating – for the security guards. When it goes black inside my bra you can hear the scuffle and everything they say. Mum went ballistic and headed off to the cop shop wanting justice. Next stop, our MP and the local paper.

All the anti-arms trade groups and people Mum calls peaceniks are tweeting it and posting it and every time the phone goes I think it's from Channel Four News. If I see a sleaze ball with a camera opposite our house I might get a false passport and head for South America.

LIKE WHAT'S GOING ON?!!!!!!!!!!!!!!!!!!!!!!!!!!!!!

Daisy's not panicking. I'd say she's triumphant. "This is how the world changes," she said.

Well mine has.

****

****

Dec 29th

Great visit to Putney. Flame greeted us like Olympic medal winners. Got my old phone back. Nina can have it – late Christmas present. So now I've got all my numbers back and there were loads of messages. Yasmin sent a text the day after the *action,* which said, *Hope you are OK?*

Last time I checked that *action* had been seen by more than four thousand people.

WHAAAT?
P.S. Daisy just woke me, at 23:17. Polly wants Flame and Nina to perform the Ecocide song at a talk she's giving in London. And she wants Daisy and me to talk about what we did and why, all paid for. I'll just nod and say, "Yeah!"

I'm a bit scared but I think I can cope. Daisy says people are starting to understand about only being *part of the web of life. We didn't weave it and we can't keep destroying it…*

"Shut up," I cried, grinning. "I know this stuff! I need my sleep, you nutter!"

****
****

There isn't a diary entry after that, not for the rest of the year or the start of the next. There's a reason for that and I can hardly write it. We lost Granny Sylvie that night, in her sleep. Mireille said she ate the biggest supper they'd ever seen her put away and talked a lot about the past, especially Amelie and when she died. Mireille said she was crying through the whole story herself but Granny Sylvie just looked peaceful. The last thing she said was after she kissed Dad goodnight. "It's only ever love that matters, and I'm so sorry couldn't give you enough." As if she really knew who Dad was. Or mistook him for the husband she left in Maidenhead. We'll never know.

Dad found her late next morning, cold but almost smiling. She must have been getting ready for death because that little suitcase of hers was full of envelopes with people's names on them and Dad said they might not all be the right names. I just sobbed. I'd never cried so much in my life. I took her hair out of my knicker drawer and stroked it like a hamster.

Zac didn't really know her but I wanted to get on the train the next day and Mum wasn't sure about letting me go alone. In the end Daisy went with me, after she'd promised Mum she wouldn't go right on to Brussels to lecture the European Parliament about Ecocide Law. France was warmer than

England and the sun was on Dad's stream. There was no sign of the canoe but I told Daisy about it.

"Your granny floated off in it," she said. "That's how I like to think of death." Well she would.

The funeral was in French, in a dark, musty church with cracks, damp on the ceiling and an old stone floor that dipped. I kind of liked it even though it all sounded a bit like a spell. I wished there was enough magic to bring Sylvie back so I could say goodbye.

It was easy enough to work out which envelope was meant for me even though she'd written *my little English Amelie* on it, and a whole row of kisses. It was fat, because inside was the letter I wrote her, and a stash of English cash. The note said: *This is for you chérie, enough I hope for the most beautiful wig in the world? XX*

It's nearly Christmas again now but I haven't spent the money yet. Like Daisy said, it's not the gift that counts but the love that gave it.

I haven't grown a single hair. Now and then, when I feel like it, I go *au naturel*, and if I catch sight of my reflection the shock-horror's all *fini* now. I won't be a loser. One thing I know, thanks to Granny Sylvie, is that you don't really lose people you love. You just keep on loving them.

We might lose some beautiful places, and species, if we don't hold on a lot tighter. Daisy told me about a raised coral island called Banaba that won't survive if sea levels keep rising. It's got no fresh water but it's beautiful. And Daisy says the weird bit is that it's shaped like a bare head. The history of the islands is really interesting and sometimes bloody, with lots of greed and exploitation thrown in along with a missionary called Captain Walkup. I found a story set there, a kind of fable called *The Goddess*. Even though it's just been written by an author friend of Daisy's with Alopecia, it feels like it's out of time. But I hope those islands aren't. And the story's weird but I'm getting to like it as much as Daisy does. You can read it too. Nei Bubura's a much better heroine than me.

I'm used to Val and the *menagerie* we live in. And I'm planning a party for when Flame comes home from uni. Ed and Nina will probably spend the whole of it glued to each other, whispering. Turns out Ed Carter only needed a friend or two to get through. I still love Flame, in a big brother/hero way, but I'm with John now. He lost his mum, Debbie, four months after we got together, but he knows he can talk about her to me. I haven't forgotten the way she asked me to *look after him* and it turns out that's something we can do for each other.

The earth needs us to look after it too and we saved one wildflower meadow. When I heard Polly say Ecocide Law can change everything, it changed me too. Because it's so easy to accept the worst, and shrug, and get your kicks out of booze and shoes and white sand – so easy, it's *normal*. But it shouldn't be so hard to believe in a better future. Daisy's convinced we're a year closer. She keeps saying the world really is turning: towards love, peace and justice – and let's face it, with her around, it's got no choice. There's no way she'll give up, not on islands like Banaba or anywhere else.

And someone has to help her.

The Goddess

1

Nei Bubura woke before the sea. It breathed no louder than her sister in sleep.

Nei Bubura woke before the sun, while the sky was still purple. Each night was hotter and shorter. Her people thought she had no fear. They trusted her, and like the pandan tree, their faith must bear sweet fruit. Nei Bubura was blessed. She was their queen, their holy one. The young men shaded their lowered heads from the light of her beauty.

But the rain so rarely came, and when it did, it teased the people out to paddle below the clouds with their coconut shells. The harder they pushed through spray in their canoes, the faster the rainclouds fled.

First to rise, Nei Bubura drank in the morning but her throat was dry. Her sister's hair clung like seaweed to rock. It caught salt and sand. It soaked up heat. As Nei Bubura stepped lightly past, she lifted one cool hand to the top of her smooth, bare head. It was her father who said the island itself was the shape of it, in the eyes of the birds above. And no one asked him how, without flying, he knew.

Purity was what he saw. A pearl, unblemished. Clear and fragrant as fresh water, she was their goddess. She must guide them through life and beyond where the dreams led on.

2

Nei Bubura had been afraid, at first, of the air that found her skin. Without hair her head had seemed small, like a nut with no shell.

Is it me, she thought? *Am I who I was? Was I always a goddess, in hiding, growing up as one of them?*

They were questions she never asked the father who placed a crown of whitest flowers around her head. *What if I am just a girl after all?*

Now, without her father, she gave her own answers. She had been born among them to understand their fears, their vanity, their greed and sadness. But it was the hair she had lost that set her apart. It was a sign and a promise.

The soles of her feet were tough; the sand was fine and white. Nei Bubura looked up to the sky that was her birthplace. Purple would bleed into blue and the sun would glare through the breeze to scorch the rocks.

Nei Bubura lifted her head and raised the palms of her hands out above the waves towards the breaking dawn.

Closing her eyes, she imagined rain on her tongue, tapping on her scalp, running down her cool, dry cheeks.

The goddess willed it.

If not today, then tomorrow.

Her power could not fail.

3

The coral island was green beneath the blue, and Nei Bubura liked to sit in the shade of the windblown palms when the sun was fiery. Propped by roots reaching out of the earth, the trees grew heavy with fruit. Papaya, breadfruit and mangoes turned from green to yellow, orange to red as they ripened. The juice would soon be thick and sweet and Nei Bubura's tongue would be the first to taste it.

But without rain the sweetness was empty.

Each morning, out on the saltwater no one could drink, Nei Bubura's brother and his friends caught the fattest fish. Each evening, Nei Bubura was first to be served around the fire, and only when she opened her arms to invite her people to join her in the feast did they begin to eat. No one went hungry.

But the taste they craved above all others was water.

Now beneath the soil, Nei Bubura's mother feared for the pumpkins. They were struggling to swell in earth that grew grittier and more powdery with each dry day.

Nei Bubura smiled her thanks to the girls waving palms to cool her skin. She could rest no longer. It was time to dance.

Through the sound of the sea and wind she breathed the lightest notes she knew. Her body bent and curved, leaned and swayed under a roof of pandan leaves. The girls who attended her danced around her. From around the island others came. Men, women and children, they bowed their heads as they moved. The black hair of women lifted like wings and flew.

But the head of Nei Bubura was unadorned and free. Like a blood moon in the night, the bare scalp rose clear and high above the rest. The movements of the goddess were slow and graceful, her steps soft on sand. She arched her arms, crossed them and scooped up air. She stretched her long body as if to find the clouds and pick them. Her steps were quicker now. She flickered. She whirled like a tornado. Inside her head she felt the heat gather. The island tilted. Her feet faltered.

Enough.

High above their heads the men carried her, and laid her down in the shade. The youngest, Kakiaba, felt too moved to look on her queenly face. With her eyes closed, Nei Bubura sensed his presence. Thinly she heard their voices praise her.

How great, they said, *was her sacrifice. How beautiful her spirit. How pure her heart.*

And when the rain fell, they would dance again. They would give thanks to the goddess who loved them, the queen who had thrown their weapons in the ocean so none might be afraid.

Nei Bubura closed her eyes. A fire burst above them and the droplets on her mouth had the salt tang of sweat.

Let it rain.

4

Later that day the breeze grew fidgety. Nei Bubura felt her people's eyes on her as the air cooled and rainclouds darkened on the horizon. Silently the islanders set out coconut shells, row on row, like farmers planting seeds.

Nei Bubura waded into the sea, arms high. Her people stood behind her, waves washing their ankles, waiting for the rain to meet them. But they could only watch from a cruel distance as a blurred sky ran soft and wet, but out of reach.

Nei Bubura felt their disappointment like a scourge on her flesh.

"It will come," she told them.

In the night she thought she heard it, greeting the rocks with kisses. But perhaps it was just a dream. In the morning the coconut shells lay empty.

The boy who loved Nei Bubura saw the sadness in her eyes and felt the weight of her burden. Sometimes he thought she was only a girl, different from all others, finer and purer in her beauty. Kakiaba wished he could hold her hand and stroke the contours of her queenly head.

As she walked proudly ahead, her wide, dark eyes on the sky, Nei Bubura heard his footsteps among the rest. Sometimes, even for a goddess, it was hard to believe.

5

Through the day the heat grew thicker and the air thinner. Nei Bubura's small sister grew weak and pale. Nei Bubura could only stroke her forehead and wave a green palm over her warm, dark hair.

She heard the wind scratch and tug, no more cooling than smoke. It smacked the rocks and made sand fly.

Nei Bubura had no eyelashes and her fine eyes stung. The island had no rivers, lakes or streams. The pools that bubbled up after rain lay dusty now. But she walked to each holy, life-giving spot and there she planted the bare feet of the goddess. Out she breathed her pure, sweet breath into the scouring wind. Though she had little strength she found enough to sing. Around her, the people echoed her song.

When the pools shone wet, it was her duty to guard them. Now she could only fill them with hope. And the gift was not enough. It would rain, very soon now. It must.

On her tongue she imagined the taste of Kakiaba's kiss. But she dared not meet the eyes of the boy who loved her. Nei Bubura was afraid that in them she would see reflected her own doubt.

Instead she walked out to a rocky ledge leaning over the waves. She stilled her heart and dived. It was her smooth bare head that met the water first, scattering the fish. She plunged like a dolphin, streamlined and strong under the surface. Above her the light danced, starry. Nei Bubura was cool now. Her silk scalp rose up and out of the sea, and air filled her lungs.

See the queen of the ocean, she heard them marvel. *How she glides. How the rocks bow before her and clear her path. How the creatures of the sea gaze in awe on her beauty.*

But Nei Bubura could not escape the drought in saltwater. She could only soothe her skin and grant herself a moment's peace from duty. Up to the sky she looked but its blue only dazzled. Even the goddess blinked away from the sun.

There was no wishing back the girl she used to be.

6

Striding onto the shore, Nei Bubura ran her hand over her forehead and down to her long, bare neck. There the queen's gold coral lay, the rarest of all, with its own inner light.

There was no one like her and she must not forget it.

Sometimes she dreamed of strange men coming, men with washed-out faces. They wore heavy clothes to hide skin like fresh guano. And they watched with hunter's eyes. Nei Bubura saw the island stripped to dry bone, and water grey with poison.

She did not tell her people what she saw. But she feared that in those dreams she glimpsed a time to come, a time so far ahead no boat could reach it.

Only the shoulders of the goddess were broad enough to bear such burdens. Nei Bubura smiled on her people as she walked tall among them. Gently evening shaded Banaba, the *hollow land.*

Watching her, Kakiaba wondered whether the goddess he loved felt the restlessness of her people. A fly buzzed around the mango he sucked even though its flesh was not yet soft and pulpy. The taste was bitter but sometimes it was hard to wait.

Nei Bubura had no wish to see another day melt into darkness without rain. Every morning the waiting grew harder as her people squinted fearfully into the light. But they must not hear her sigh. Again she walked onto the shore and let the waves that traced its edges wash her feet. Above her, the colour was draining from the sky.

But surely it was too soon for darkness to scud in. It must be rainclouds that seeped, far away, through the faded blue. Somewhere showers were falling, and striking the waves that tossed them away.

Behind Nei Bubura a boat was tied to a rock. She heard it rattle with coconut shells as the wind licked around and bumped them. The men hung back, waiting for a word from the goddess. But this time she would not watch them bob away and chase in vain. It was for her to race the rain, and there would be no failure, no defeat. The wind would not challenge her. This time it would not drive the clouds away.

Kakiaba was first to drag the boat onto the water. Nei Bubura nodded her thanks and stepped on board. Taking the paddle, she steered a way out towards the grey skies, her bare head sprinkled by the spray. Foam whitened the crests of the waves whipped by wind. Her arms worked like a man's, their rhythm strong. She was a queen and she would save her sister. She would save them all.

7

On and on Nei Bubura paddled as the sea deepened with every stroke. Its swell was powerful, but so were the long arms of the goddess. Seawater speckled her cheeks and trickled down her bare head. But it was the touch of rain she longed to feel and now she could sense its freshness on the wild wind. The rainclouds could not be far away. Though the horizon outpaced her, slipping always beyond her grasp, the grey clouds above her drew near. They flowed towards her like a vast river with no bed.

As the waves reared, Nei Bubura felt the boat lurch. A sudden growl broke from the sky. A sharp needle of light pierced the cloud. And the rain fell on Nei Bubura, washing her bare head, her shoulders, her breast. It chinked and splashed in the coconut shells. Breathless, she let it fill her gaping mouth. But the wind was against her now, twisting the sea and lifting it high around her. The shells clashed and fought as the sea tried to break in and seize them.

See her battle, she imagined her people cry. *See her courage and her strength. See the goddess overcome the storm.*

8

In her dream the people bowed to a pale man in black with a ring of white around his neck. The pages of fat black books were turned by wind but the shower that sprayed them was red.

Waking, Nei Bubura felt no power in her limbs. She was not kneeling but lying, limp as a dead fish.

Opening her eyes, she saw feet encircling her. Sand clung to her body, cracking as she moved. Looking up, one hand shielding her face against the sun, she saw strange faces. The shouts she heard around her head were jagged, harsh. If they held words, she did not know their meaning. But she understood the message of the big male hand with fingers spread towards her. *Stop.* Or *No.*

These were not her people and the shores she glimpsed through squinting eyes were wider, rockier and more ragged than home. She had been carried like a fruit across the sea to an island she did not know. On the air she smelt the rain that had fallen here. But this was not Banaba and here she was no queen.

Staring down on her, the faces were not respectful. Nei Bubura felt their eyes on her sandy head, and suddenly it felt naked and small. She reached to brush the wet specks from her skin. Had the rain blessed her people too, on Banaba?

These strangers had feasted on water. But she heard no thanksgiving, no rejoicing. A finger jabbed towards her. The voices clashed. Someone laughed. Their heads were straggly with hair, every one of them, but they were not in awe of her beauty.

Nei Bubura flinched as a large foot prodded her, as if she were a crab that might be alive, not dead. Salt encrusted her gaping mouth and stung where the skin tore. Voices thudded hard around her like drums. Now arms grabbed hers and dragged her till she felt herself tugged onto her feet. The gold coral was torn from her neck.

She felt dazed, unsteady. They pulled her, and both legs sagged beneath her. Weakly, her head too light to hold high, she stumbled, and the light drenched her.

Nei Bubura sank onto sand.

9

They had put her in a cage. The roots of a pandan tree had been tied together to trap her but the sun and breeze burst through the spaces between them. There was no room to stretch, or even stand. She bent her head down and held her knees.

Someone had heard her moving. Quick, light footsteps rained towards her. Pointing, children giggled. Their dark hair glinted with salt and their skin was wet from the sea. One boy picked up a twig, and pushing it between the gaps in her walls, prodded her below her neck.

Another child was on haunches staring in at her with narrowed eyes. He reached in and pulled at her ear. The rest laughed loudly.

Nei Bubura's chest swelled with proud indignation. Lashing out with both arms, she beat against the roots but they did not snap. She only snagged her skin. Blood trickled free.

"I am the goddess Nei Bubura," she told them. Her voice sounded firm and steady even though her heart felt wild.

Again they laughed. A handful of sand flew in her face. She spat and her raw eyes watered.

At a rasping yell the children ran. Nei Bubura heard the tread of a strong man, two. They were coming for her. But her gaze must show them she was not afraid.

One man waved his knife like a palm. Nei Bubura looked on it with dull disdain, and turned away, head high. With a sudden flick he sliced the root closest to her head. Through the opened space he pressed the sharpened coral blade between her breasts.

Nei Bubura glared, not at the knife but the man. Looking away, he withdrew. Then he threw his head forward and spat. As the spittle struck her scalp, they jeered. She felt it run warm and slow on her skin but she would not touch it. The sun would snatch it away.

Pulling a grotesque face, he rubbed his thick black hair, waggled his ears and lolled out his tongue. Nei Bubura did not understand the words he threw at her but she knew what they meant. She was not only different but less. Her bare head filled them with fear.

They were leaving now, but they would return. And they were too afraid to let her live.

10

In her dreams the coral bled. Running red, the island was a graveyard, a killing field. Along a flat rock path, a huge bird with no feathers rolled, whined and took flight. The sky was fiery and the earth roared. And all the men were dressed the same, walked with the same rhythm, spoke with the same tongue and closed the same eyes.

Once again Nei Bubura shook herself free of sleep but still it held her in its power. She blinked and firmed her spine as upright as the cage allowed.

A breadfruit, sliced in half, lay just out of reach. A gift from a child, perhaps, who took pity on the strange bareheaded woman in her trap? Taking the stick used to bait her, she leaned one arm out between the roots and stretched her muscles tight, tighter. At last the twig touched the rough skin of the fruit, batted it, tipped it closer.

She smelt the man before his shadow muffled the sun. He picked up the fruit, one half in each hand, and dug in with his teeth, circling with his tongue. Nei Bubura turned away until she heard the fruit discarded on the sand. The man was shouting and beckoning. Others ran towards her.

The snapping roots were loud in her ears. Armed with knives, the men attacked the cage till it fell like firewood around her. But not for a minute did she think herself free. The voices made no music as they joined, competed, struck. Hands grabbed, but this time they raised her high, flat above their heads – like a body cold once the spirit had flown.

Nei Bubura did not look up where the sun blazed but she heard the cries of the petrels and the urgent, bat-like flutter of their wings. Her head burned but she breathed in the breeze, the rain's freshness lingering on it. The fear was theirs, not hers. With her dignity she would make them understand.

She did not struggle as they tied her to a wild almond tree spreading white and pink against a sun-drained rock. When they snagged her flesh she made no sound. Her dry mouth formed a smile as she gazed on the bright beauty of the flowers. In her imagination Nei Bubura crunched the hard, sweet almonds she could not reach.

A calling tern speared over the water to dive. In her mind's eye Nei Bubura flew with the bird, out to sea and home. Lashed to the trunk, her dress no longer stirring, she straightened her neck and felt her pride return. She knew their eyes on her bare head, their pointing fingers and jeering speech, could not diminish her.

Now they brandished knives and spears, only to curve them around her on the sand, a vicious necklace and a threat. But still she was not afraid. Smiling, she showed them love. In the silence that spread among them, and stilled the air, she felt a power that brightened her eyes.

Soon they walked away. But the last of them, a boy who reminded her of Kakiaba, splashed her face with the rain caught in a coconut shell. Her heart surging, Nei Bubura blessed him with a murmur on glistening lips, and a nod of her cooled head.

11

For Nei Bubura, time had lost its shape and rhythms to the heat and hunger. Sleep had made her forget. Now she woke to find the soft edges of darkness cloaking the rocks, sea and sky. From her scalp to her gritty toes, it chilled her skin. A flurry of breeze shook an almond from a branch, but hard as Nei Bubura tried, bird-like, she could not catch it with an open mouth. Her tied wrists were torn.

Perhaps she would sleep again if she closed her eyes. Nei Bubura told herself she must, or she would shiver till her teeth chinked like the coconut shells in the storm. Maybe if she pictured the pools on her own island, bubbling to cool her sister's fever, the gladness of her people would keep her warm as the night grew black and cold.

Soon, between sleep and waking, she glimpsed bats, their eyes like black stars and their wings scuffling. Above their dance, the moon began to peel open like a ripe fruit. It heartened Nei Bubura with its gentleness and she bowed her head in thanks.

Through her weariness the waves began to chatter. A stirring, low. Had they come to kill her now? Stiffening, she would not crumple. Girl or goddess, she was Nei Bubura. She was different but she was not ashamed.

Something moved, quick and light. Not a crab or a rat. A tall shape, with breath that echoed her breath, warm on the night air.

As she felt herself untied, she thought she glimpsed the contours of a face she knew. The boy who reminded her of Kakiaba! He had slipped away to free her. But no! If he betrayed his people he would pay with suffering. Nei Bubura shook her head. She asked for no sacrifice.

"Nei Bubura."

It was a voice she knew, his voice. Kakiaba! The boy who loved her had come. Slowly she followed as he led her by the hand. Soft as two lizards, they stepped over the weapons towards the waves. In one hand he picked up a spear from the menacing chain, and sent it speeding towards the horizon. Then another. Two more, one in each hand, plunging gently into the waves. And again and again, light and sharp as rain.

And it had rained! She could see it in his eyes. She could smell it in his hair. Nei Bubura reached for his hand. Lightly, as if in a dream, she felt herself guided into the boat. His lips brushed hers.

"The rain came," she said. "I rejoice for my people."

"Only when Nei Bubura returns," he said, "will her people rejoice."

Sitting, she received a shell full of water, and as he began to paddle, she closed her eyes and drank till it filled her with delight.

Calm waves welcomed them. Nei Bubura heard nothing but the soft strike of the paddle through dark sea. Her strength returning, she reached out her arms. Pushing the paddle towards home, she saw only the white foam and the thin, smoke-grey outline of the boy who loved her. Remembering his kiss, she felt the touch of moonlight on her skin.

"Your queenly head is crowned in silver!" Kakiaba cried. "And I thought you were a girl after all."

"I am," she said, and laughed.

"I can't tell what you mean," he said, and in his voice she heard him smiling. "A goddess or a girl?"

Nei Bubura leaned her silvered head towards his mouth and kissed him.

"I am," she said.